TRUE STORIES
IN SIX GENERATIONS

HANNAH'S
Girls

Elaine
(Born 1961)

Ruth Vitrano Merkel

REVIEW AND HERALD® PUBLISHING ASSOCIATION
Since 1861 | www.reviewandherald.com

Published by Review and Herald® Publishing Association, Hagerstown, MD 21741-
1119

Review and Herald® titles may be purchased in bulk for educational, business, fund-
raising, or sales promotional use. For information, please e-mail
SpecialMarkets@reviewandherald.com.

The Review and Herald® Publishing Association publishes biblically based materials
for spiritual, physical, and mental growth and Christian discipleship.

The author assumes full responsibility for the accuracy of all facts and quotations as
cited in this book.

Texts credited to NKJV are from the New King James Version. Copyright © 1979,
1980, 1982 by Thomas Nelson, Inc. Used by permission. All rights reserved.

This book was
Edited by Penny Estes Wheeler
Designed by Patricia Wegh
Cover art by Matthew Archambault
Typeset: Goudy 13/16

PRINTED IN U.S.A.

11 10 09 08 07   5 4 3 2 1

Library of Congress Cataloging-in-Publication Data
Merkel, Ruth Vitrano.
  Hannah's girls : Elaine / Ruth Vitrano Merkel.
      p. cm.—(True stories of God's leading in six generations of Adventist girls)
   Summary: In the 1960s when Elaine and her family move back to Grand Rapids,
Michigan, they return to a new home, neighborhood, and friends, along with their fa-
miliar Adventist church and its members.
[1. Family life—Michigan—Juvenile literature. 2. Seventh-day Adventists—Juvenile
literature. 3. Friendship—Juvenile literature. 4. Christian life—Juvenile literature. 5.
Grand Rapids (Mich.)—History—20th century—Juvenile literature.] I. Title.
   PZ7.M5363Han 2007
   [Fic]--dc22
                                    2007039074

ISBN 978-0-8280-1955-2

Dedication

To my daughters,
Elaine and Marcia,
&
To my grandchildren,
Erin, Benjamin, and Bradley

Other books in the *Hannah's Girls* series, by Ruth Vitrano Merkel:

Hannah's Girls: Ann (1833-1897)
Hannah's Girls: Marilla (1851-1916)
Hannah's Girls: Grace (1890-1973)
Hannah's Girls: Ruthie (1931-)

To order additional copies of
***Hannah's Girls: Elaine* (Book 5)**
or other books by Ruth Merkel, call 1-800-765-6955.

Visit us at www.reviewandherald.com for information
on other Review and Herald® products.

Contents

Introduction

This fifth book in the *Hannah's Girls* series finds Ruthie now the mother of two girls, Elaine and Marcia. The girls' family has just moved to Grand Rapids, Michigan. It's a move back home for Elaine and Marcia, though they're moving to a different house and a different street from where they had lived before.

The girls hope that there are nice kids on their new street, and there are—except for Monica. She's tough. She's mean. And even though they try to like her, they can't. Until quiet, shy Joanie does something that changes things.

Camp meeting is the highlight of their summer, and this year is no different. Come with the girls. Listen to the boys' teasing, and sing along with them all to the tunes of "Old MacDonald" and "Oh, My Darling, Clementine." Crouch with Marcia and her friends behind the brush as they wage war on the people who pass by.

Family is important to Elaine and her sister, even though they've never lived close to their cousins or grandparents. Join them at their family reunion. Listen to Grandpa's stories from Sicily. Meet Elaine's cousin who was in the Army in Vietnam. And wonder with Elaine why Grandpa seems so much older and frail.

This true story is Book 5 of a six-book series.

—*Ruth Vitrano Merkel*

Hannah's Girls Family Tree

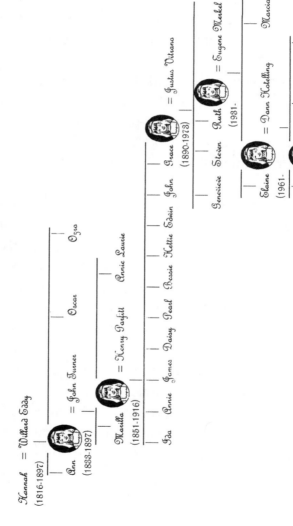

Hannah = Willard Eddy
(1816-1897)

Ann = John Turner
(1838-1897)

Marilla = Henry Parfitt
(1851-1916)

Ida | Annie | James | Daisy | Pearl | Bessie | Hattie | Edwin | John | Grace = Justus Vitiano
(1890-1978)

Annie Laurie

Oscar | Ozro

Genevieve | Steven | Ruth = Eugene Merkel
(1981-)

Elaine = Dann Natelborg | Marcia
(1961-)

Erin | Benjamin | Bradley
(1988-)

Generation Five

Elaine
(Born 1961)

ERIN'S MOTHER

Some of the people you'll meet in Elaine . . .

MARCIA: Elaine's younger sister.

JOANIE: The first girl Elaine meets when they move to Grand Rapids. They quickly become friends.

CINDY: Another new friend on Elaine's block. Cindy has a large, friendly dog.

MONICA: A tough, rough girl who lives on the same street.

DON AND JUDY HAM: Friends of their dad. Elaine and Marcia had a big surprise at their house.

UNCLE STEVE: Elaine's uncle, and a Bible teacher at Andrews University.

ROGER: Uncle Steve's son. A year and a half older than Elaine, he's good at baseball.

GRANDPA AND GRANDMA VITRANO: Elaine's grandparents on her mom's side. They live in California but every year come back to Michigan to stay awhile near their son, Elaine's uncle Steve.

DON AND RICK: Grown-up cousins from California. Don has just returned from war in Vietnam.

JERRY FORD: A congressman Elaine and Marcia waved at when they saw him in a local parade. He later became president of the United States.

ONE

New House, New Kids

Elaine plunked herself down on a chair and looked around her bedroom. *H'mmm, it's beginning to look better—a bit more settled. Lots better than yesterday! Moving is a chore, just like Mom said it was.*

Elaine had her clothes all hung in the closet: dresses with dresses, pants with pants, and tops with tops. She'd just finished putting socks, underwear, cards, some pens and pencils, and a jewelry box in her old chest of drawers. She had taken care that the drawers were neat and orderly, too, at least for now. They probably wouldn't stay that way forever, but she'd given it her best shot.

The biggest change was that now she and her younger sister, Marcia, had their own bedrooms. In fact, she could hear Mom helping Marcia set up her play table and chairs, and Marcia was saying, "I think I'd like my Lite-Brite on the table for now." That was Marcia's favorite game. Grandma and Grandpa had given it to her for Christmas, and she loved making pretty color pictures with the glow pegs.

Their new home was in a quiet neighborhood on a short street that ended in a turnaround.

"There won't be much traffic," Dad had explained

when he told them about the new house he'd just found for the family. They were moving 50 miles, so Dad had gone up ahead and found a house. "Little traffic means more safety, so I'm sure you girls will like living on that street."

They'd been living in Kalamazoo, Michigan, while Dad finished his Master of Business Administration degree. Now he'd become a partner in a Grand Rapids, Michigan, certified public accounting firm. Dad had a new office to move into as well as a new house, so once the moving van was unloaded, Mom and the girls worked at unpacking and putting everything in place.

They all thought it was good to be back in Grand Rapids again, for that's where they'd lived before moving to Kalamazoo. Elaine already knew the kids she'd be with in church and at church school, but now that they were in a new neighborhood there'd be new kids to meet.

Elaine sat on her bed, daydreaming. There was a far-away look in her eyes. She was thinking about the advice Dad had given them when he told them they were moving back to Grand Rapids—but not to their old house. Dad had grinned when she and Marcia had asked if there were nice kids in their new neighborhood. "I can't vouch for that. I didn't meet the kids," he had said, tousling Marcia's hair. "But this I know—good kids are always looking for other good kids to play with. There are only about a dozen houses on our street, counting both sides, and I'm sure there are some very nice kids in those nice houses. You'll just have to wait and see. Put your best foot forward. That's a good motto to remember. After all, you don't get a *second* chance at making a good *first* impression!"

Elaine and Marcia had laughed at that. They knew what he meant.

Elaine wasn't a bit shy, but moving someplace new where she didn't know a single soul was a little scary. At least at first.

"And always remember," Mom had added, "a nice smile goes a long way."

Dad had pulled both girls into his arms with a warm squeeze. "At least we're not moving to Timbuktu," he'd teased. "We're just headed back to Grand Rapids."

The sisters had raised their eyebrows and looked at him. They'd never heard that strange name before.

"Where on earth is this Timbuktu place?" Elaine had asked. She wondered if he'd made it up to tease them.

"It's over in Africa, somewhere," Dad had said. "Now, that would be a place to visit someday." Dad was full of fun.

"Timbuktu," Elaine had whispered. It was fun to say. But in Africa? That was really far away. She wondered if Africa was even farther than Japan.

Elaine got up, stretched, and headed for the kitchen to get a drink of water. Mom was putting dishes in the cupboards. "Things are beginning to take shape," she said when Elaine came in. Mom stood on her tiptoes to reach the highest shelf with some plates they didn't often use. "Thanks to your good help, I can see the light at the end of the tunnel." She patted Elaine's shoulder. Elaine worked right alongside Mom. She put the silverware in a kitchen drawer, helped her unpack towels and stack them in the bathroom closet, and helped make up the beds. And that was just for starters!

Now looking past Mom's shoulder, Elaine saw their front yard through the living room's bay window. There was that girl again. The day before, she'd stood on the corner opposite their house, watching the van being unloaded. Elaine wondered if she lived there. She could just be visiting her grandma or something. The girl was kind of short and thin, and yesterday she'd timidly raised her hand and waved when Elaine looked her way. Elaine had waved back.

Now Mom turned and saw the girl too. "You can go outside and meet her if you want," she said, nodding toward the window. "Just don't go far. I may need your help again."

Elaine didn't need telling twice. She scooted out the door and across the street. "Hi," she said with a big smile. "As you can see, we just moved in. My name is Elaine."

"My name is Joanie," the girl said. "I saw you and, I guess, your sister."

"Yeah, the other girl is my sister." Elaine tossed her thick blond hair from her face. "She's younger than I am. Are there any other kids around here?"

Joanie leaned against her mailbox. "Several kids. And two other girls about our age."

"Oh, that's—" Elaine started to say, but someone interrupted.

"Yeah, *me*!" said a loud, deep voice.

Elaine spun around to see who it was. This girl was nearly a head taller than Joanie and just bigger all over. "I'm Monica," the girl said, "and don't you forget it." She dragged her foot along a crack in the sidewalk and pointed with her thumb. "I live down thataway."

"Nice to meet you," Elaine said politely, remembering Dad's advice. "I'm real glad there are girls my age on this street."

The three stood awkwardly for a minute. Somehow having Monica there changed everything. So Elaine said that she'd better get back home. Monica grinned and poked Joanie in the side with her elbow. "Ya better get back in your house, too. Your mama probably wants to see if your hands are still clean."

"Well, 'bye." Elaine turned and ran back home, glad to get away from Monica. She'd never met anyone like her in her whole life. That girl was rude. No, she was worse than rude. She was hateful. Elaine felt sorry for Joanie, but she knew one thing. She wanted to get to know Joanie better, but she wasn't at all sure about Monica.

That evening, just before supper, Elaine was in the garage looking for the box that held all their puzzles. There were still a lot of things to do, and she didn't want to lose track of the puzzles. Just then she saw a girl with a dog on a leash walking by, so she stopped her search and skipped down the driveway to meet her.

"Hi," the girl said. "I see you just moved here. My name's Cindy." She and the dog had stopped at the edge of the driveway.

"I'm Elaine." She stood a few feet back from Cindy. "Is your dog friendly?"

"Sure. He's friendly. His name is Pal." Cindy came a step closer. "You can pet him if you want."

Elaine held out her hand palm upward, as Mom had taught her to do. Mom said that dogs didn't seem to be afraid of people who approached them with an open hand, but a hand held palm-down was an indication that the person might hit them.

Sure enough, Pal slowly moved forward and gently sniffed Elaine's open hand. Then he gave her fingers a little lick.

"Guess that answers your question," Cindy said with a crooked smile. "He's old, but gentle and friendly. He doesn't always like everyone, though."

"What does he do if he doesn't like you?" Elaine asked. She was wondering if he bit.

Cindy laughed. "Oh, if he doesn't like you, he just ignores you. But it seems he likes you."

Elaine couldn't help asking, "Does he like Monica?"

Cindy's laughter was like great bells. She understood exactly what Elaine meant. "Naw, he just ignores her. Same as I do."

"Just how many kids live here on this street? I know there's you, Joanie, and Monica."

"Kerry and Scott live across the street. And Rusty lives there," she said, pointing in the direction of a nearby house. "They're all younger than we are, and so is Sandy, who lives down near the turnaround. But Sandy has a swimming pool in her backyard. Isn't she lucky!"

"Oh, yeah! That'd be neat. I know how to swim some, but I want to get better at it." Elaine bent down and stroked Pal's head. "I have a younger sister named Marcia. Do you have any sisters or brothers?"

Cindy grinned. "Oops, I almost forgot to tell you about them. My big sister, LuAnn, graduated from high school just a couple weeks ago. She won the Miss Congeniality contest last year at school, and this summer she's gonna work in Chicago, where she has a job with CoverGirl Cosmetics. She'll live with our aunt Lorraine and uncle Howard in Westmont. That's a Chicago suburb. She'll have to take the metro line into work. Boy, is she excited!"

Wow. That was a lot of information. Elaine thought it all sounded really neat. "Your sister sounds nice. Do you have any brothers?"

"Just one. Jeff. He's a couple years older than I am. You'll like him," she said. "Everybody does."

"Thanks for the rundown," Elaine said. She could see that Pal wanted to get on with his walk. "Hope we see lots of each other."

Cindy smiled. "Me too. Sometimes it's fun to sit down in the park and visit. We can have fun there just talking and doing nothing,"

"The park? Where's that?" Elaine asked, looking up and down the street. She didn't see any park.

Cindy pointed back toward the street's end, just where the road turned in front of her own house. "See that empty kinda grassy area across from our house?" Elaine nodded. "Well, that's what we call the park. It's nothing special, but it's a place to kinda hang out. We usually sit on those short tree stumps. An older man named Mr. Van Denburgh owns the property. He keeps the grass mowed, and he doesn't care if we kids play there as long as we don't dig holes or get too rough on the land. No ball games or anything. Mrs. Van Denburgh grows some raspberries nearby, closer to her house. The large field beyond the grassy spot is owned by a man who keeps it planted in alfalfa or soybeans or something."

"That sounds fun. I think I'll like the park."

"And I'll take you down to the old variety store on 28th Street, too," Cindy told her. "It's got candy, gum, milk, bread, pop, kitchen stuff—lots of other stuff. Jeff's friend Davy works there some. It's owned by Mr. and Mrs. Morgan, but everyone calls them Harley and Hatty. Actually, not everyone," she laughed. "My folks won't let us kids use their first names. My dad and mother say they are top-quality people. The Morgans never had any children of their own, and maybe that's why they like having kids drop in."

Elaine had never met anyone who talked as fast as Cindy and gave as much information. It almost made her head spin, but it was fun. "Wow," she said, "thanks for the info. I almost feel that I know the people around here just by listening to you."

She must have lived here all her life, Elaine thought as Cindy and Pal walked on down the street. And that's how Elaine and Cindy became friends. ✾

TWO

It's Great to Have Friends

"Tonight we're having dinner with the Dodds," announced Mom the next morning.

"Yippee!" the girls cheered.

Jim and Natalie Dodd were dear friends of the family. Dad and Jim had been business majors in college, and that's how Mom had met and become close to Natalie. The Dodds lived in a lovely old farmhouse not far from Grand Rapids.

"Natalie knows what it's like to move," Mom told Elaine and Marcia, "so she's trying to make our life a bit easier by fixing us a good, nourishing dinner. That's something I haven't had time to prepare lately."

As soon as they drove in the Dodds' driveway, Mrs. Dodd opened the door to welcome them. Elaine thought that she must have been watching out a window.

"Jim just called and said he'd be here real soon," Mrs. Dodd said after giving Mom and the girls a hug. "So while we wait I'll show you what we've done to the house." She linked arms with Mom, and Dad and the girls happily followed. Natalie, as Mom called her, pointed out the newest improvements made to their old farmhouse. Years before, when they'd moved into their "new" old country home, they had decided to do some renovating. The

19

kitchen was drab, so Jim—Mr. Dodd—decided to put in new drywall. To their surprise, when the old drywall was removed, they discovered that the original kitchen had been made of logs. So instead of covering the logs up again, Mr. Dodd rechinked between the logs.

Dad looked at it closely. "Jim did a great job with this," he said, running his fingers along some of the chinking. Once again the old house could boast a charming, old-fashioned kitchen.

"I love it, Natalie. It's beautiful," Mom told her. "Who would have guessed that this old house held the secret of a log kitchen? It's a little like living in a log cabin."

In this new "old" kitchen was a delicious supper, almost ready to be eaten. It smelled wonderful. Fairly soon Mr. Dodd arrived from his work. Everyone hugged again, and when they were all seated at the table, Mr. Dodd thanked the good Lord for His protection over all of them since they'd been together last.

"Amen!"

Dad, Mom, and Mrs. Dodd said amen at almost the exact same time Mr. Dodd did. And everyone chuckled.

"They're close like family, aren't they?" Marcia asked as they drove home. She'd had a good time.

"Indeed they are," Dad said. "Jim and Natalie are wonderful friends."

Gradually Elaine and her family settled in to the house and neighborhood. Every day things got better. Dad had put up the swing set in the backyard and emptied some more boxes. Now he could park both cars in the garage. Mom was almost finished sewing the window curtains for the girls' bedrooms, as well as the dust ruffles and canopies for their beds. It was quite an undertaking, but Mom loved doing it.

Now both girls had new bedspreads for their new white bedroom furniture. The bedspreads were identical, but they weren't the same color. The spreads each had small, flowery designs, but Elaine's was a light, airy yellow and Marcia's a soft, delicate green.

The new double dressers had large mirrors, and the nightstands next to their beds were topped with knobby, milk glass lamps. The girls thought their rooms were beautiful.

"Ooohhh," said Elaine as she ran her hands over the new bedspread. "I love it, Mom. The tiny flower design makes me think of summer. Thanks."

"Let's look at my room," urged Marcia, leading the way. Marcia spoke softly as she stood at the foot of her bed. "My light-green bedroom reminds me of spring, I guess. And Mom, the canopies are so pretty. I've never seen anything like this. My whole bedroom is beeeautiful." She threw her arms around her mother. "Thank you, thank you, thank you."

Mom smiled at each of them. "You are certainly welcome. I must say, I like your rooms myself."

"Your mother has good taste," said Dad later when he came home from work. He crossed Elaine's bedroom to look out her window into the backyard. "I'm going to have a chain-link fence installed around our backyard," he said. "I've been thinking about it. It will be a safety measure, and that way, if we should ever get a dog the fence will be up and in place already."

"A dog?" squealed Elaine. "Did you say a *dog?*"

"A dog?" repeated Marcia. "A *real* dog! Goodie, goodie gumdrops."

"I didn't know you had that in the back of your head," Mom said with a grin. "I'd love to have a dog. Not a big one, but a dog is such good company and such a good pet."

"We'll just wait and see. Someday the opportunity might come along, and we'll be ready," Dad smiled. And that ended conversation about getting a dog.

⚜

At supper Mom said, "When I was sweeping the driveway this afternoon, I met Kerry's mother. It's nice to start getting acquainted with our neighbors."

H'mmm, Elaine thought. *Maybe Mom wants to be acquainted in the neighborhood just as I do.* That was something new to consider.

"I met Joanie's mother, too," Mom went on. "She told me that next week swimming lessons are going to start at the YMCA. She's thinking of having Joanie take lessons, but Joanie's a bit hesitant and, actually, so is her mother." Mom passed the plate of corn on the cob to Dad, who took a second. "Elaine, would you like to take lessons?"

she asked. "I know you already know how to swim, but lessons would help you get even better."

Elaine almost jumped off her chair. "Would I? You bet I want to take swimming lessons!"

"So do I. So do I," Marcia chimed in

"Well, the class for children your age will be later, Marcia," Mom told her. "But yes, you can take lessons too. It's just that you won't be with Elaine."

Marcia's lips turned down at that, but she didn't say anything, and Elaine was too excited to notice. "We'll think of some fun things to do while Elaine's in swim class," Mom told Marcia. "And your time will come soon."

After helping with the dishes, Elaine biked down to Cindy's house to tell her about the swimming lessons.

"Oh, brother!" said Cindy. "I'll be gone visiting Aunt Millie in Muskegon this next week. Otherwise I'd take swim lessons too. My mother is going to help Aunt Millie wallpaper her three bedrooms. Sorry, Elaine. I'd love to be with you and learn how to swim better."

On her way back home Elaine saw Mom talking to, of all people, Monica's mother. Quickly putting her bike in the garage, Elaine slipped indoors. She went to the bay window to watch so she'd know when the conversation ended.

Elaine ran to Mom as soon as she came in. "What's happening?" she asked. "What was Monica's mom talking to you about?"

Mom smiled and explained. "I was getting the mail, and who should come out but Monica's mother. We spoke for just a bit. As I sorted through the mail, the topic of swimming lessons came up. She said she was going to have Monica join the class too."

Mom's eyes twinkled. "If Monica is anything like her mother, I can understand why you don't feel comfortable around her. A bird happened to fly over as we had our brief talk, and one of its droppings landed on her mailbox. Monica's mother's vocabulary is something else. To say that she can swear like a sailor would be absolutely true, and I've heard sailors swear!"

Elaine couldn't help giggling. "Like mother, like daughter?"

Mom wagged her head. "What a tongue that woman has. But the upshot of the whole thing seems to be that both Joanie and Monica will be taking lessons when you are."

"Oh, brother. Monica too," said Elaine, but then her eyes brightened. "Of course, there will be other kids to meet." She tried to console herself. Maybe Monica in a larger group wouldn't be too bad.

The phone rang the next morning after breakfast, and Elaine heard Mom say, "Hi, Kathleen." Then she heard one side of an excited conversation. Elaine knew that Kathleen LaTour and her doctor husband, Frank, had been friends of Mom and Dad's since they'd all been in college together. Even though a lot of time had passed, the families had stayed in contact. Both went to camp meeting every year, so they saw each other then, and sometimes they'd even vacationed together.

Mom had sat down with a glass of orange juice to enjoy visiting with Kathleen. Elaine could tell that they were discussing camp meeting, and that was always exciting. So she went to find Marcia to give her the news. Marcia and Kerry were swinging in the backyard.

"Marcia!" she called. "Mom's talking to Mrs. LaTour about camp meeting."

Marcia jumped from the swing and ran with Elaine into the house. "So long, Kerry," she called with a wave. "I'll come back after a while." So Kerry kept swinging. She didn't have a swing in her yard, and she loved playing with Marcia. In fact, one day Kerry's mother playfully asked her if she planned to move in with Marcia since she spent so much time with her.

Elaine and Marcia stood as close to Mom as they could and still be polite. They didn't want to miss any camp meeting detail she might say. "Oh, yes, I turned in our application months ago," they heard Mom say. "Back in January. I asked for a tent next to yours, as usual."

Marcia and Elaine clasped hands and lightly jumped up and down together. Mom was still talking. "OK. That's good . . . Yes, we're all moved in here. I wish you could come see us . . . Talk to ya later. 'Bye." Mom hung up, but before she could say a word to the girls, the phone rang again.

"Oh, hello, Mother," Mom said happily. The girls knew immediately she was talking to her own mother, Grandma Grace. This would take awhile, so Marcia went back out to swing with Kerry, and Elaine sprawled out on her bed to read a new book Aunt Gen had sent, *Caddie Woodlawn*.

Aunt Gen was Mom's one and only sister. She lived all the way out in California, where she taught at the La Sierra elementary school. She and Uncle Bob had two sons, Don and Rick. Elaine didn't know those cousins very well since they were a lot older than she was, just as Aunt Gen was quite a bit older than Mom. But Aunt Gen and Mom had always been very close, and Aunt Gen, being a teacher, kept Elaine and Marcia up-to-date with interesting children's books to read. She sent them play clothes, too. She was an excellent tailor and made many of her own clothes. With the pieces of fabric left over from her projects she'd make play clothes for Elaine and Marcia—cute tops and pants or shorts.

Later, after she'd talked to Grandma Grace, Mom explained that the LaTours were going to attend Michigan camp meeting. "Kathleen was just checking to make sure that we'd sent in our application," Mom explained. "And guess what she suggested? She told me to compose a camp meeting cantata. She really got a kick out of the birthday poem I wrote and sent to her last April."

"Do that, Mom!" Elaine exclaimed. "You're good at poetry. I'll bet it would be great." Elaine was enthusiastic, but suddenly she stopped. "How do you *do* a cantata?" she asked.

"It's nothing more than writing a long poem, and I just might do it," Mom said. "I'll write words to be sung to music that already exists. I'm thinking of everyday songs or tunes that we all know. That's right up my alley." She grabbed Elaine's hand and spun her around the kitchen.

"Oh, before I forget, Grandma and Grandpa are now at Uncle Steve's place. She just wanted to let me know they'd arrived safely."

Mom sat down on a chair and drew a deep breath. "It seems that my folks are growing older so very fast. Especially Grandpa. He's getting feeble and a bit stooped, and his walk is unsteady." She shook her head. Elaine thought she looked sad. "Of course, he is in his 80s," she went on, almost talking to herself. "I cherish any time I can spend with him—with both my parents, for that matter." She had a pensive look on her face.

During the winter Grandma and Grandpa lived with Aunt Gen in southern California. It was much warmer than Michigan, and unlike Michigan, it didn't have any snow. But during the summer they returned to their apartment at Uncle Steve's.

Elaine caught Mom's reflective mood and began thinking about her elderly grandparents. "One time I asked Grandpa why he drummed his fingers on the arm of the chair while he rocked, and you know what he said?"

"What?" Marcia asked. She'd come in from outside to hear about camp meeting too.

"He said he was humming a tune in his head, and his fingers were keeping the time. He laughed, and I asked him what tune it was. Right away he said, 'When the Roll Is Called Up Yonder.' Then he said, 'Let's sing it together,' so we did. He has a nice voice, doesn't he?"

"And I like the crinkles around his eyes when he smiles," Marcia said, "and he hugs tight, too."

"No tighter than Grandma!" Elaine laughed. "She says she comes from a huggy family."

"Both my parents love music," Mom told the girls. "In fact, it was through music that Mom and Dad met." The girls knew this story, but they liked to hear it again.

"Mother played the piano for the evangelistic meetings Dad held when he first was sent to Milwaukee. Back then he was a young new minister right out of Broadview College. And Mother was living in Milwaukee with my aunt Bessie and uncle Charlie while she attended business school." Mom had that faraway look on her face again.

"Even though Grandpa's hair is thin and gray now, it still shows the wave he once had," Mom said. "He keeps it combed back and doesn't let it get straggly. My mother's hair still curls a bit around her face. Everyone in the family had wavy hair, except me." Mom pretended to look forlorn, but the girls knew she was kidding.

"Grandma was glad to hear that you're going to take swimming lessons, Elaine. She never learned to swim, and neither have I, but we agree that it's important to know how to swim. It may save your life or someone else's life one day."

Elaine had never thought about that. Saving a life sounded significant. Would she ever do a thing like that? What would it be like?

❧❀❧

The first week in their new home went by fast. On Sabbath Elaine was excited to be going to church and seeing the friends she hadn't seen for a year. The church building was familiar to the girls, and they knew just where to go for their Sabbath school classes.

As soon as Marcia went into her classroom Suzie waved and pointed to the chair next to hers. Marcia quickly sat down, and the girls grinned at each other. Then Kathy came through the open door and took the chair on the other side of Marcia.

It was easy for Elaine to join her old crowd too. She no sooner had entered her Sabbath school classroom than Janet, Barbara, Jamie, and Denise jumped up to meet her. Terry, Nick, Brent, and Chris joined them.

"You look just the same, Elaine," Barbara squealed, "even though we haven't seen you for ages!"

"It's only been about a year, Barb," Elaine laughed.

"But you've let your hair grow longer," Janet said. "I like it that way." Then turning slightly, Janet continued. "Elaine, this is Missie. She and her family just moved here." She pulled the new girl into the group. "Missie, Elaine used to live here, and now she's moved back."

"Today's my first Sabbath back," Elaine told her.

"Hello," Missie said with a shy smile.

"And I'm her older brother, John," spoke up a good-natured boy, throwing back his shoulders—standing straight as a military officer. He gave Elaine a cocky smile. "Pleased to meet you."

The other boys laughed with him. "Hi, Elaine," they all said.

"Glad you're back. I'm just as tall as my brother now,"

Terry announced, striding toward Elaine so that she could notice his height. He lightly tapped her shoulder. "You'll have to look up to me now!"

"And now that he's cut his hair short," said Nick, "we can actually see his"—he paused dramatically—"his eyes!" Nick was always a cutup, although truth be told, Terry was never on the short end of the stick when it came to mischief-making.

Brent grinned and said, "Hi, Elaine. Glad you're back."

Good-natured Chris smiled and bowed toward Elaine as if he were a proper Englishman. And before the kids could talk anymore, their leader stepped up, and Sabbath school began.

Elaine took a chair among the girls. It felt so comfortable being back. It crossed her mind that Mom and Dad always talked about the good times they had at college and academy reunions, and now she knew what they had meant. Coming back to her old Sabbath school and all her friends made her feel the same way.

When church was out, it seemed that everybody stopped to visit with Mom and Dad. Elaine was happy to see that they were introduced to Missie's parents. Their names were Don and Irene Ross, and their family had been living in Africa, where Don was a missionary doctor.

At last they all piled into their car, Mom and Dad in the front seat and Elaine and Marcia in the back. The girls were talking about all the kids they'd seen when Dad said to Mom, "You know, the Rosses are good folk. I'd like to become better acquainted with them."

Mom nodded. "So would I," she said. "Irene told me that they're here in Grand Rapids only temporarily while Don does some specialty training at the hospital. We'll have them over for dinner real soon."

A few days later Cindy, Joanie, and Elaine rode their bikes down to the park and sat there relaxing and talking. They pulled up blades of grass and tried blowing and whistling through them the way Jeff and Davy did.

By now, Elaine had met Cindy's brother, Jeff. She thought that he was just great. Not only was he fun, but he was good-looking, too. In her mind she compared him to her cousin Ed, Uncle Steve's older son. She always had fun with Ed.

Elaine pulled up another blade of grass and said to her friends, "I should know how to do this grass-blowing thing. My dad showed me." So trying again, she placed the long blade carefully between her thumbs and blew real hard. A loud, wobbly bleat of a whistle *yeowled* through the air, and the girls burst out laughing.

"Now show *us* how," they yelled.

"OK, but first, have a treat on me." Elaine put her hand in a pocket and pulled out several small Tootsie Roll candies she'd tucked in there before she'd left the house. So they all chewed and talked and teased each other. Cindy put a blade of grass to her mouth and tried to whistle, but she couldn't even make a sound. Joanie and Elaine laughed and laughed. "Finish your Tootsie Roll first!" Elaine sputtered around the last of the sweet she had in her mouth. "Finish your—"

"*What's cookin'?*" boomed a voice from behind them. They'd been laughing so hard that they hadn't even noticed Monica come walking down the road.

"Oh, nothing," Joanie said. Cindy couldn't talk. She was still giggling.

Monica's eyebrows scrunched together right above her eyes. He mouth was a perfect upside-down *u*. That girl could look meaner than anyone they'd ever seen. The three friends got quiet in a hurry. No one said anything at all.

Then Elaine broke the silence. "Here, Monica, have a Tootsie Roll," she said, gently tossing the little wrapped candy to Monica. She caught it in midair.

"Hey, thanks, Elaine!" Monica looked surprised.

"Good catch!" Elaine replied.

Elaine wasn't certain whether Monica noticed the lag in conversation, but soon restless Monica got up to leave. "Well, 'bye, you sissy-missy girls."

Cindy gave Monica a withering look. "Oh, why don't you just go home and tell your mother she's calling you!"

Monica didn't look back, and as soon as she was out of earshot, the girls giggled. "Where did you come up with that expression, Cindy?" Elaine asked.

Cindy shrugged and smiled. "I heard my brother say it. Why in the world did you give her any candy, Elaine?

She's probably never shared anything with anyone in her entire life."

"Well, I dunno. I really feel sorry for her, even though I get mad at her. But then I stop to think. I don't want to be like her—ever—and I wonder if she *ever* wonders what it would be like to be nice. Maybe the candy will make her sweeter."

"Yeah, right," said Cindy. "*That's* an impossibility!"

"Well, last week in Sunday school my teacher talked about the golden rule," said Joanie. "That's just what you did now, Elaine. You were nice to Monica the way you'd want someone to be nice to you." Joanie was a loyal and gentle friend.

"Guess so," reflected Elaine, lying back in the soft grass and stretching her arms above her head.

THREE

Making a Splash

 On Monday morning Elaine couldn't wait to jump out of bed. Swimming classes began that afternoon, and she wanted to be ready. Pulling on a pair of shorts and a T-shirt, Elaine went into the kitchen and found Dad finishing his breakfast. "Today's the big day, huh?" he said.

"Yeah. I can't wait."

"Well, you have fun in swimming class. Pay attention and learn all you can." He pushed back from the table and handed Mom his empty juice glass. "When we were boys, your uncle Fred and I, with our friend Don Ham, walked clear downtown to the YMCA in Davenport, Iowa, so we could take swimming lessons. Imagine, three miles all the way to the Y, and then three miles all the way back."

"You *walked?*"

"Yup. We walked." Dad winked at Elaine. "We really wanted to take swimming lessons."

Mom patted Dad's arm. "You love the water, don't you?" she said. "You're a sailor at heart."

Dad nodded. "Like Popeye the sailor man," he chuckled. Then he was out the door.

"Your dad would not have been aboard a ship if it wasn't for me," said Mom lightheartedly. "Imagine. In the Navy, but never on a ship."

"That's 'cause he was flown to the naval base in Japan in an airplane. Right?" asked Elaine. She'd heard the story before.

"Yes, it was peacetime after the war in Korea, so wives were allowed to live with their husbands overseas. I worked in the same hospital as Dad did. And when he was discharged, we came home on a troop ship. Wow, did he have fun! He was out on the deck every day."

As Mom retold the story Marcia had come into the kitchen, rubbing her sleepy eyes. "Were you scared over there, Mom?" she wondered aloud.

"No. Everyone was nice to us. Even though we couldn't communicate easily, a smile is a smile in any language, isn't it?" That saying was a favorite of Mom's. "Our Japanese neighbors were always pleasant. They had no more to do with World War II than those of us who lived in the United States. That was the doing of their warlords. By the time Dad was stationed there, the war had been over for several years, and the U.S. military was known as the occupation forces. It wasn't scary. We felt very safe."

"Those pictures you have of Mount Fuji are real pretty," Elaine said. "They're interesting, too."

"Mount Fuji is a beautiful mountain, I must say," replied Mom. "On clear days when we walked along the shores of Sagami Bay—that was only a couple blocks from our house—we could plainly see Fuji in the distance. We never got to climb it, though."

"That would have been fun," Marcia said. She liked to climb things.

"Well, I can't remember if I've told you this or not, but Dad and I got to see Japan's Emperor Hirohito."

"Who's he?" asked Marcia.

"The emperor is like our president of the United States. One of Hirohito's summer palaces was in our town of Hayama. It was surrounded by a high wall, and guards were placed every so often around it. They'd smile when we took their pictures, although we didn't try to bother them too much."

"Boy, Mom!" said Elaine. "You've been around the world! Well, almost."

"One afternoon when we were out walking on the beach after work, the emperor's private yacht sailed in. He took great interest in the study of marine life and had been out exploring with an American marine biologist."

"What?" Marcia squealed. "Hirohito was a marine?"

"No," Mom laughed. "He enjoyed observing sea life—fish and whales and the like. Immediately the guards asked us to keep a good, long distance away as the emperor disembarked. The guards were polite, but we knew we'd better obey. Of course, we were glad to. We didn't want to cause any trouble. Fortunately, Dad had his camera with him, so he took a picture of Hirohito. Imagine! We saw an emperor before we had even seen a president of the United States. Dad and I were very excited."

"Was he wearing a crown or whatever emperors wear?" asked inquisitive Marcia.

Elaine threw back her head and laughed. Her little sister could be so funny.

"No," Mom replied. "As I recall, he had on a short-sleeve shirt, with tan pants like the ones your dad wears. He had a canvas hat on his head. Of course, if this had been an official occasion, he would have been dressed up."

"I can still count to five in Japanese, just like you taught me, Mom," Elaine told her.

Marcia spun around in a flash. "Tell me. How do you say it?" Her eyes were wide with excitement.

"*Ichi, ni, san, shi, go.* Right, Mom?" Elaine looked at her mother for approval.

"Correct. You have a good memory. That's how the American kids would count before they began a race. Instead of saying, 'one, two, three, go,' they'd repeat the Japanese words. Cute, eh?"

Marcia looked at Elaine, and they both laughed. "I won't forget that, Mom," giggled Marcia. "*Ichi, ni, san, shi, go.* I'll always remember it. Wow! I can say something in Japanese!" She was tickled. "Just wait till I tell Kerry."

Now that Mom was in a Japanese mode, she continued. "Japan's national flag is a simple but stunning one. It features a round red circle on a completely white background. The circle represents the sun—the 'land of the rising sun,' which is a symbolic name for Japan."

"Why is that?" Elaine wondered.

"Well," Mom explained, "we all say that the sun rises

in the east and sets in the west. So since Japan is farther to the east than most other countries in the world, its flag with the round red globe represents the rising sun."

"That's neat," Elaine said.

Marcia nodded too. "That's cool," she said.

"Now I'll teach you a common Japanese greeting. To greet someone 'Good morning,' you nod and say, '*Ohayo.*' It sounds as if you're giving the name of the U.S. state of Ohio. Those in the military and other Americans there quickly learned that word."

"That's clever," Elaine laughed.

"Class dismissed," Mom chuckled as she reached into a kitchen cabinet for three bowls. "Now let's eat." Elaine got the breakfast cereal from the cupboard, and Mom put out blueberries, bananas, and toast. While Marcia set the table Mom poured orange juice for them all.

The YMCA pool was the biggest pool Elaine had ever seen. She watched with wide eyes while she stood in line with Mom waiting to register for the class. Joanie and Monica with their mothers were right behind them.

"Doesn't this look exciting!" Elaine told her friends. "I can hardly wait to get in the water."

Monica nodded agreement and clumsily bounced on her toes. Joanie looked concerned.

Elaine quietly turned to Joanie. "Don't worry," she said. "We'll have fun."

"I hope so," said Joanie with a quiver in her voice.

Joanie's mother looked worried too. "I know just how Joanie feels," she told Mom. "I never learned to swim myself, but I do think she should give it a try. If she doesn't like it, she can quit."

"I don't want *my* daughter to quit," Monica's mother boldly declared. She was a large, opinionated woman who loudly expressed her mind. "This will help keep her busy and out of mischief this summer, at least for a while." She frowned down at Monica and rapped her on the head.

With a jerk Monica pulled away. She looked at Elaine and rolled her eyes. Elaine felt a little funny. She was sure glad that her mom didn't fuss about her in front of people and didn't rap her on the head. On the other hand, Monica was a handful, and Elaine never wanted to be on the wrong side of her. One thing was certain: Monica never, never bothered with Cindy. Elaine knew full well it was because of Cindy's big brother, Jeff.

Elaine remembered saying to Cindy, "Monica never gets anywhere bossing you around."

"She'd better never try," Cindy retorted. "I've had to tell her off a time or two. Now she avoids me like the plague, and I'm glad she does!" Cindy's eyes had brightened as she spoke. "I'm glad she's not in my room in school. I'll bet her grades are all wet."

"What's that mean—'all wet'?" Somehow Elaine figured it was a joke.

"They're probably all below C level." Cindy chuckled. "Got that one from Jeff."

I bet Monica knows she'd have to pay the piper if she ever tangled with Cindy, Elaine thought. But poor Joanie was always on the receiving end of Monica's teasing.

Standing there in line, Monica now glared at Joanie with a look of disgust.

"Don't be a sissy, Joanie. You're always such a scaredy cat," she said with a self-important tone in her voice.

Joanie sheepishly hung her head, then turned to look at Elaine.

Without even a glance at Monica, Elaine took Joanie's arm. "You can be with me, Joanie. We're gonna have fun."

Joanie's mother saw and heard the girls' conversation and looked gratefully at Elaine's mom. "I hope this will work," she said weakly.

Now it was Mom's turn to offer encouragement. "Don't be disturbed. Not yet, anyway. You may find that you are pleasantly surprised. Joanie may just come out of her shell and do well in the water."

The two women smiled at each other.

"Humph," growled Monica's mom as she turned her back on the other mothers.

After registration, the girls hurried to the girls' locker room, where they could change into their swimsuits. And their mothers left to run other errands, as parents were not encouraged to stay by during the lessons.

Monica's mother scurried off immediately, but Joanie's mother hesitated, walking out to the parking lot with Elaine's mom.

"Elaine is such a sweet girl," she said before getting into her car. "I'm glad Joanie has Elaine to lean on. Before you folks moved to the neighborhood she had no one her age to play with except Monica."

"Didn't Cindy join in the playtime?" Mom asked.

"No. Cindy didn't come down the street toward our place until you folks moved in."

Mom understood and nodded her head.

"But Elaine and Cindy have given Joanie a boost this summer. Just in the short time that you've lived here I've begun to see a difference in her. I see a bit of self-assurance she didn't have before," Joanie's mother said.

"Keep on encouraging her," Mom advised. "She needs to know that you believe in her."

After slipping into their swimsuits, Elaine, Joanie, and Monica hurried back to the pool area. Several of the other swim students were already there.

When all the kids had arrived, Jack had them sit on the edge of the pool while he stood in the shallow end. At this point, they weren't even allowed to dangle their feet in the water.

"Listen up, everyone," he called. His voice echoed against the walls. "My name is Jack, and this is my helper, Jill." He pointed to a perky-looking girl standing in the water near him. All the kids laughed to hear that their teachers' names were Jack and Jill.

Jack grinned and waited until the laughter died down.

"I know how strange that may seem to you, but I can guarantee you that these are our real names and that we did not go 'up the hill for a pail of water.'"

More laughter.

"You are the biggest class we've had in quite some time," he continued, "so I want your strict attention when I show you how to do the different strokes, kicks, and maneuvers."

By now all eyes were focused on Jack. Then he had them line up one behind the other and one by one jump in to him. Once they were in the water, he had them hang on to the side of the pool and kick their feet. Jill was there to help anyone who was unsure of what to do.

When it was Joanie's turn to jump, she just couldn't do it. She stood by the pool, her toes a little ways from the edge. She looked so scared that Jack said she could sit back down and watch for a bit longer. While she watched, he and Jill went to each child to check their skills. Some of the kids did really well hanging on to the side and letting their body float in the water while they kicked their feet. But some needed a little help.

Then Jack had the students stand in the shallow water and duck their heads under the water. Oh, there was a lot of sputtering and laughter. Elaine confidently followed all his instructions. After all, she already knew how to swim a bit. She noticed that some of the kids were definitely more advanced than others, but they were all there to learn how to swim properly.

Now and then Elaine looked up at Joanie, and Joanie

would give her a little smile. After Jack and Jill had worked with all the other kids, Jill helped Joanie ease into the water. Then supporting her in her arms, Jill walked around the shallow end of the pool, splashing water on her face now and then. Joanie laughed and loved the attention.

When Mom returned to pick up Elaine, she found her bubbling over with excitement.

"Oh, it was fun," Elaine told her. "Our teacher's name is Jack, and he reminds me of our cousin Edwin."

"Did Joanie like him?" Marcia wondered.

"We all liked him right away," Elaine explained. "And Jack's helper is a cute girl named Jill. She looks about his age. Jack says we're the biggest class he has had in a while. There were quite a few of us."

Marcia giggled at the names Jack and Jill. "That's just like the old Mother Goose rhyme," she said.

"Yeah. It is kinda funny to have those two names. Jack let us laugh, but then he kept our attention and went right on telling us what he wanted us to do."

"It was nice of him not to force Joanie to do what she feared doing," Mom said. "There's no need to frighten her right to begin with."

❧

Each swim day was better than the day before. Elaine became friends with a happy, carefree girl named Lynn, who was as eager to learn to swim as was Elaine. Then unexpectedly, Monica dropped out of class. She came by Elaine's house to tell her that her grandmother in

Traverse City was seriously ill and she had to go with her mom to take care of her.

Actually, it turned out for the best. Elaine and Joanie didn't miss her, and Joanie was beginning to be more relaxed in the water. Without being taunted by Monica she made real progress. Now she would even stand in the water by herself, jump up and down, and twirl around. But she couldn't muster up enough courage to try any strokes just yet.

"Joanie doesn't enjoy the water the way I do," Elaine told Mom after class one day. "She doesn't want to try any strokes unless Jack or Jill are right beside her. Jack told her today that she had to try a little harder or she wouldn't be able to pass the class, so she did make some effort."

"Joanie is such a nice girl, but she is a timid soul, it's true," Mother said. "Some people just seem to be born that way."

"It's just as well that Monica's gone. At least now no one there makes fun of her," Elaine said. "Today toward the end of class Jack asked Joanie to kick her feet while she held on to the side of the pool. She did—for the first time—and we all cheered. She grinned real big. I think she was proud of herself."

"That oughta make her feel good," said Marcia. "I think I'd like Jack."

"Well, Lynn and I are willing to try everything Jack asks us to do," Elaine said. "She says that we'll be the stars of Jack's class. I like her. She's older than I am, but she doesn't act stuck-up about it."

The last day of swimming class the parents got to sit in the bleachers and watch their children perform. Elaine and the other children could jump in and swim clear across the pool. Jack had each child do an underwater somersault and float on the water facedown. Some did better than others, but they all tried. Even Joanie, probably encouraged by her mother being in the audience, jumped into the water, held on to the side of the pool, and kicked. Then Jill put her hands under Joanie's tummy and walked her across the pool while Joanie tried stroking and kicking. All of a sudden Jill let go, and Joanie swam—for the first time. She was ecstatic. Her mother pulled at Mom's arm. She was speechless but grinning from ear to ear.

To end the performance Jack announced that some of the children had learned to jump from the diving board. Mom was happily surprised to see Elaine and Lynn join the small group of boys that walked down to the deep end of the pool. While Jack treaded water beneath the diving board, he had each child jump from the board. When they came to the surface, he'd give them a gentle shove, and they would swim to the side of the pool.

Marcia's eyes lit up at this. "Did you see her, Mom? Elaine was in the deep end! She didn't tell me about this."

"I know, I know," Mom said proudly. "Wait till Dad hears about this!"

The students all huddled around Jack when he got out of the water, and he went from one to another, giving each a handshake. It was obvious that he had won their hearts and confidence.

"You did well, Elaine. You're going to be a strong swimmer. You passed with flying colors. And so did you, Lynn," he said and again shook their hands.

When he came to Joanie, he said enthusiastically, "Just think, Joanie; I saw you swim all by yourself." Then he explained to her that if she would continue to practice, he was sure she would pass the class next time. She gave him a shy smile, ducking her head and whispering, "Thank you." Then everyone was dismissed, and the girls ran to the locker room to change into their clothes.

"'Bye, Lynn; it sure was nice to know you," Elaine said as she waved to her new friend.

"I wish we lived nearer to each other. We'd have fun. 'Bye!" And Lynn waved a friendly farewell.

That night when Dad came home, he took his three "girls" out for ice cream so they could celebrate Elaine's success. Dad always called Mom one of his "girls," too.

FOUR

Roger's Glove and Grandpa's Stories

On a Sunday afternoon Elaine heard a car pull up in the driveway. She quickly ran to the window. "It's Uncle Steve and Aunt Charlene, and they have Roger and Grandma and Grandpa with them," she called.

Uncle Steve and Aunt Charlene lived in Berrien Springs near Andrews University, where Uncle Steve taught classes in the seminary and Aunt Charlene taught business classes in the academy. Elaine thought Uncle Steve actually looked like a professor—dignified and scholarly. Petite Aunt Charlene always had a plan for their get-togethers. What an organizer she was! *You'd have to be well organized to be a teacher*, Elaine thought.

The girls ran out to meet them, and Roger almost jumped from the back seat before Uncle Steve could bring the car to a stop.

Roger, just a year and a half older than Elaine, was her first cousin. She thought that Roger's brown hair spilling over on his forehead and his sparkling blue eyes made him a handsome boy indeed.

Mom and Dad came outside too, and everyone hugged everyone, all talking at once.

"You girls have grown so much," said Grandma as she gave each granddaughter a bear hug.

"And it's such a nice day for a visit," Mom said, giving Grandma an extra hug. "It couldn't be nicer weather for the drive up here."

"It's *so* good to see you," said Grandma. She stood back and looked at her daughter.

"Yes, and Grandpa, too," Mom said, hugging him again.

"Hi, Roger," Elaine said. "Wish Joyce and Edwin could've come."

"There wasn't enough room in the car," laughed Roger, "or they might have." (Joyce and Edwin were Roger's older sister and brother.)

Elaine noticed that Grandpa walked deliberately and carefully, but his smile was as loving as ever. Uncle Steve held his arm as they walked to the front door. But Grandma hadn't changed much—she could still hug like a bear.

She'd been slim and trim all her life, and now, in her late 70s, she still carried herself with grace and quiet charm. She wore her gray hair pulled back loosely in a French twist, but little wisps of curls escaped here and there and framed her face.

As they made their way into the house, Elaine looked at her grandmother's hair. "Your hair is still fluffy," she told her.

Grandma squeezed her hand. "So you remember me telling you how I could comb my hair into the latest styles when I was a girl?"

"Yeah, and how the girls would tap the top of your

head to see if you had a 'rat' under there to keep your hair so puffy. Isn't that the right word, 'rat'?" Elaine grinned as she looked at Grandma.

"Yes, 'rat' is right. It sounds awful, but it was just a soft pad that girls tucked under their hair to make it stand high and fluffy on top," Grandma explained.

"That girl, Nola, was the stuck-up one who patted and checked your hair the most, wasn't she?" Elaine couldn't help chuckling at the memory of the "uppity" girl Grandma had told her about in her own school days stories.

Grandma chuckled too and again squeezed Elaine's hand. "You have quite the memory." They were at the front door by now. Dad waited there, holding the door open.

"Welcome. Come in to our humble abode," said Dad with a sweep of his arm. He had a big smile on his face.

"Oh, we're so glad you came," Mom said as she hugged both her parents again.

"We thought it would be fun to see your new home," Grandma told her as she looked around the living room and then into the kitchen. "And I see it is just as nice as you said it was."

"It's getting there," replied Mom. "We're enjoying it so much."

When everyone was settled, Elaine couldn't wait to tell her news. "I just passed my swimming class at the Y, and I can jump in the deep end and swim to the side."

"Congratulations!" everyone cheered.

"She really does well," said Mom proudly. "I want her to be able to be a strong swimmer. Someday it may save her life, or the life of someone else. You never know."

Saving someone's life. The thought took root in her brain and her heart. *Will I ever save someone's life?* Elaine wondered.

"I'm glad you've learned to swim, honey," Grandma said. "I never enjoyed water much, even though I lived just a block from the Wolf River when I was a girl in New London. My father owned and operated an excursion boat, so I had plenty of opportunities to be *on* the water, but I was rarely *in* it."

"Mother," Mom said, "I seem to remember a tragic drowning accident in our family a long time ago. Wasn't it your aunt who drowned?"

"Sit down, everyone. Here comes a story," Dad said with a nod.

❧

"It's not a terribly long story," said Grandma, "but it truly is a sad one."

Elaine, Marcia, and Roger hovered around her as she sat back in the easy chair. "Well, my aunt Mary Turner and her family were enjoying a holiday at Pelican Lake. That was north of Antigo toward Rhinelander, a place they liked to go boating and swimming. We lived in New London, quite some distance away, so no one in my immediate family was there.

"Somehow, one of Aunt Mary's children, my cousin Tillie, fell out of the boat. I can only guess how frightened both Tillie and Aunt Mary were. I imagine that Tillie was thrashing around in the water, screaming and crying. Aunt Mary must have been desperate, for she jumped in the water to save Tillie." Grandma sighed. "Neither of them could swim, and they both drowned. I'm not quite sure what happened next, but a third little girl drowned also. Aunt Mary and Tillie are buried in Antigo, Wisconsin."

She looked at Elaine. "So you see why it's important to learn to swim."

Everyone nodded. What a tragedy! Even though it had happened many years before, it still made Elaine feel strange to hear the story.

Then it seemed that all the grown-ups were talking at once, so Elaine and Marcia went outdoors and sat with Roger in the sunshine on the front step. The girls loved Roger. He was the only cousin their age in Mom's family, and he was fun. Of course, being a year and a half older than Elaine, he was taller than she was. He was a very active, well-mannered boy.

"You always have great jokes," Elaine said as she sat down. "Catch me up on the latest. Know any new ones?"

Roger raised his eyebrows and cocked his head while he thought for a moment. "Yeah, here's one. How do we know Abraham was smart?"

Elaine thought for a minute, then frowned and shrugged.

"Because he knew a Lot," Roger explained. Grinning, he said, "Here's another one. "What did one ear say to the other?"

With a big grin, Elaine came right back at that one. "I didn't know we lived on the same *block*."

"You're right, Elaine!" Roger shook her hand. "OK, then, how about this one? What did one wall say to the other?"

"Don't know," Elaine and Marcia chorused.

"I'll meet you at the corner."

Elaine groaned and put her forehead in her hand. Marcia rocked back and forth, giggling.

"Here's the last one I can think of. Why do humming-birds hum? You're gonna groan at this one, too, Elaine. The answer is, because they don't know the words."

Elaine laughed. "That's cute, Rog."

"Yeah, thanks, Roger," Marcia echoed. Then head tilted, her face screwed up, she asked, "Where'd you get all those jokes, anyway? I never hear any good jokes."

"A friend of mine at school got them out of some book in the library, I think he said. Anyway, they're kinda corny."

"I think they're funny!" Marcia told him.

Roger jumped up. "Hey, I got something to show you," he called as he ran to the car. He came back with a new baseball glove, so, of course both girls had to try it on their hands. It was heavier than any other glove they'd ever tried—huge and stiff and thick. They just couldn't figure out how to use it.

"How does this thing help anyone catch a baseball?" Elaine asked, laughing at her clumsiness.

Roger stood up and took the glove from his cousin. Easy as pie, he slipped his hand into the glove, punched it in the middle like a pro, then jumped into the air, pretending to catch a high-flying baseball.

"You make it look so easy," Elaine said with admiration.

Roger, like his brother, Edwin, was good in sports, and he had a good sense of humor. Ed had graduated from Andrews Academy, and he planned to be a PE major in college. He was really good at sports,

"So you like swimming, eh, Elaine?" asked Roger. "I love it too."

"It's important to know how to swim," Elaine said with a nod. "That was a really awful story Grandma told about her aunt Mary, wasn't it?"

Roger agreed. "But swimming is lots of fun, too. The thing is that you have to be careful. I guess back then, when Grandma's aunt and cousin drowned, there weren't life jackets. But today no one should go on a lake without a life jacket."

Just then Mom came to the door and said, "Come on in, kids. Let's have some lemonade, and maybe Grandpa will tell you a story."

"OK," the three said in unison.

They didn't have to be coaxed. Story time with both Grandpa and Grandma was fun. Grandpa's stories of his life back in Sicily were always interesting and exciting. Elaine took two glasses of lemonade from her mom and gave one to Grandpa. He was sitting in the big, soft rocking chair with his feet on the stool. *He's still a good-looking man,* Elaine thought. She could see how Grandma would have taken a "shine" to him, as she sometimes said.

*I'll bet he was a good-looking boy, too. Kinda like Roger, with
the same brown hair and handsome blue eyes.*

She'd never forget the story of Grandpa as a boy,
scolding and yelling at a grown man who was beating a
dog. And how mad the man got at Grandpa and began
chasing him. When Grandpa saw his tall, strong uncle up
ahead, he ran straight to him and hid behind his legs,
peeking out to see what the mean, horrid man would do
next. Now, the uncle knew what kind of guy the man was,
and he believed his nephew, who was crying as he hid behind his legs. "He was beating his dog, Uncle, beating his
dog!" Grandpa had said again and again. So his uncle told
the man to go home and behave himself instead of pick-
ing on kids and dogs! That part of the story always made
the girls laugh. Yes, dear Grandpa loved animals.

"Now, then," said Mom to her father, "I'd like for our
children to hear about your days growing up on the island
of Sicily."

"Yeah," said Elaine and Roger, and they plunked themselves down on the floor at his feet. Marcia climbed right
into his lap. All three looked at him, ready for some fun. But
Grandpa seemed lots older than he had when Elaine last
saw him. She couldn't put her finger on it, but he seemed
thinner and frail . . . yeah, that was the word, *frail*. His
glasses slid down a bit on his nose, and he just looked—frail.
She didn't want to even think of ever losing him. She
closed her eyes and shook her head. No, never!

Then Grandpa began:

"Our little town of Misilmeri was on the west side of

the island. We didn't live far from the Mediterranean Sea, but it was too far to walk there, and we didn't go very often. We had no cars. So swimming in the ocean was not an everyday event. Besides, I was expected to help my father in his large garden and in the lemon orchard. What little playtime I had I spent with neighbor boys playing soldier."

Grandma laughed and teased Grandpa, "And *you* were always the general, weren't you, Justus?"

"Yes, Grace, I was *always* the general," Grandpa said, grinning at his grandchildren.

"*General* Justus!" Roger said, saluting him with a grin.

Dad held up his hand and interrupted the conversation. Standing straight and tall like a military officer and clicking his heels together, Dad announced in his most official ship captain's voice: "Now hear this. That's not quite right, folks. It has to be General Justus, SIR! That's how to address an officer." Everyone could see the sparkle in Dad's eyes.

He went on to explain, "If we didn't say 'Sir' and snap our heels together, we were in trouble with the United States Navy."

Everyone joined in the fun and laughter.

"Yes, General Justus, *Sir*, go ahead!" said Mom, imitating Dad. "Let's hear the story."

"Justus, tell them about your venture up the mountain," urged Grandma.

"You climbed a mountain?" Elaine asked. She and Roger slid themselves closer to Grandpa's feet.

So Grandpa continued his story.

"Our town was near the base of a small mountain, and we could see the ancient ruins of an old castle near the top of the rocky slope. One day I took my 'men' on an 'excursion'—with our parents' permission, of course. It was rough going up, but we were energetic boys and didn't mind at all. We laughed and talked and hustled each other all the way up. Once at the top, we took time to look around at the old walls and stones.

"However, going down was a different story. It was harder, much harder for me. It was then I learned that I suffered from the fear of heights—something called acrophobia. Some of the drop-offs were far steeper than they'd seemed on our way up. My 'men' had to help their 'general' down the mountainside!"

Grandpa wagged his head as he finished his story, and the laughter that followed was in loving sympathy.

"Grandpa, didn't you have a ball diamond somewhere?" Roger was curious. He loved sports.

"No ball diamond and no football field. But we thoroughly enjoyed playacting that we were tough, rough-and-ready soldiers. It's the same as American boys do when pretending to be cops and robbers or cowboys and Indians."

Grandpa drew a deep breath and settled back.

"Don't stop yet, please," Uncle Steve said. "Tell us all about coming to America. I want these kids of ours to hear your adventure-filled stories."

Aunt Charlene agreed. "Oh, please do. These are an important part of the children's heritage. It's important to know where your ancestors came from." She loved stories that told of family history. Her mother's family had come to America before it became a nation, and she was a member of the Daughters of the American Revolution. Aunt Charlene enjoyed discussing family heritage with Grandma, who was very interested in her own family legacy. "Yes, we definitely want to hear your story," Aunt Charlene said, urging Grandpa on.

So Grandpa happily continued. He enjoyed telling the stories too.

"I wanted to come to America so bad that I bedeviled the daylights out of my father. When he finally consented, we crossed the ocean, and it was the greatest adventure I'd ever had before or since. Our ship, carried a little more than 1,000 passengers. All but 40 of us traveled third class down in the hold of the ship, where it wasn't luxurious. However, I spent most of my time on deck, visiting and talking to friends that were traveling with us. I never suffered from seasickness, as many of the other travelers did. The day we sailed into New York Harbor was a wonderful day. I hurried forward so that I would not miss seeing the famous Statue of Liberty."

"You saw the Statue of Liberty?" young Marcia asked in surprise.

"Yes, Marcia," Grandpa replied. "And it was all that I dreamed it would be. That day will live forever in my memory."

"Wow!" said all three kids.

"I grew to love my new homeland, and I wouldn't trade it for anywhere else in the world. Be thankful you are Americans, children. We are fortunate to live in the land of the free and the home of the brave."

Grandpa's eyes glistened, and there was silence for a moment.

"I can just see you, Justus," said Grandma with a smile, "talking to everyone on the ship. You are so outgoing, much more than I am. I don't believe you've ever met a stranger!"

"Well, that's all the stories for right now," Grandpa said, giving Marcia a hug.

"Does anyone want more lemonade?" Mom asked. "There's more in the fridge." Elaine helped Mom pour some more, and Marcia took Grandma a glass, walking carefully and slowly to her chair.

"See, I didn't spill a drop," she bragged, and Grandma gave her a long, tight hug.

The day passed far too quickly. Too soon Aunt Charlene and Uncle Steve said they needed to start back to Berrien Springs. "When are you coming back?" Elaine asked Grandma. "I don't want you to go."

"We'll be back when Uncle Steve can bring us," she said. "And maybe you can come down and see us."

There were hugs all around. Then the family watched and waved as the car backed out of the driveway, turned down the street, and disappeared from sight.

"I do like Grandpa's stories," Marcia said to no one in particular, and she and Elaine stayed outside after their parents went back in.

"I wish they didn't live so far away," Elaine said.

"Me too."

It's Always Fun
at Camp Meeting

"It's time to make our plans for camp meeting," Mom announced a few evenings later. "Time is just flying."

"Yippee!" cheered Elaine. Camp meeting time was such fun. She loved going, and so did Marcia.

The plan was that Mom and the girls would stay for the full 10 days. Dad would attend on the weekends, and if he could, he'd drive back for a meeting midweek—depending on his work schedule. That was what most of the other fathers did too.

"Another excursion coming up for us is a short trip to Colorado," Dad told them. "I'm going to attend some professional meetings in Denver, and I think I'll give my friend Don Ham a call. He pastors a church not far from Denver, and it would be fun to visit him."

"Oh, I agree," said Mom. "We'll plan on it. When do we go?"

"Not until after camp meeting."

"Is that the same guy who took swimming lessons with you and Uncle Fred?" asked Elaine.

"One and the same," Dad replied. "He was a great pal."

Mom spoke up. "Just this morning I talked again with my friend Kathleen. Both of us turned in our tent applications a long time ago. As usual, we both asked them to assign our tents near each other." She pulled a funny face. "We hope the organizers don't mess up and forget about us."

Elaine's eyes brightened. "We always have such good times with the LaTours. Their kids are fun. I like being with all three of them."

"Yeah, Cheryl's lots and lots of fun," said Marcia. "Camp meeting wouldn't be camp meeting without her and her brothers."

"Yeah, Bill and the Battle Creek Academy guys he hangs out with are always nice to me, even though they're older than I am," said Elaine. "They could be snooty if they wanted to be. Buddy Houghtaling and that other fellow who hangs around with Bill . . . Oh, what's his name?" Her brow wrinkled. "Aristotle! That's it. They're such cutups, those three, but they aren't wild boys. My friends all think they're neat."

"What a name—Aristotle," Marcia said with a wrinkled nose. "I know that's just his nickname, but what a name." Both girls giggled.

"His real name is Ron," Elaine reminded her. "But isn't Aristotle a lot more interesting?"

"Donn, the middle boy in the LaTour family, fits in real nicely too," said Mom, and both Elaine and Marcia nodded in agreement. "Friends are precious in this life," Mom continued. "Never forget that."

"Cheryl, Arlene, and I call ourselves the three musketeers." Marcia's bright eyes sparkled. Arlene was the daughter of yet another family of friends, Ruby and Cal Campbell.

So it was that when camp meeting time drew near, excitement filled the house, and Elaine cheerfully helped Mom pack. She brought up the suitcases from the basement, chose some of the clothes she wanted to take, and helped Marcia pack her suitcase. Everywhere you looked Elaine was busily involved in the preparations.

"Let's see, now," Mom said as Elaine hovered around her while she checked her list. "I have all the bedding ready and the soap and towels. The hot plate is in the garage ready to go, and I have the two coolers and the few dishes, dish soap, and pans that I always need. The rug for the tent's 'front room' is all rolled up, standing in the corner of the garage. I vacuumed it well, so it looks good."

"Don't forget the dishpan, Mom," Elaine reminded with a quirky smile. "Remember when you forgot the dishpan?"

Mom grinned and then made a long face. "Don't remind me! Dad huffed, but then quickly ran to a store in nearby Grand Ledge to get another one; but he kidded me that it was my plan all along to eat out for every meal so that I wouldn't need to wash the dishes."

"What about the broom," asked Marcia, "and the dustpan, and the folding chairs?"

"Yes, they're all out in the garage, ready to go too."

"And the cans of food you usually take—soup, sandwich spread, olives, and whatever," added Elaine.

"Yep, it's all packed. I also have my little toolbox

ready with scissors, needle and thread, thumbtacks, nails, a small hammer, and so forth," Mom added.

"It's a good thing we're taking both cars," observed Elaine. "One car couldn't hold all this stuff."

"When did you get all this ready?" asked Marcia.

"Little by little while you girls played. As I thought of the things to be done I'd collect this and that," Mom told her. "It makes it easier that way. Oh, Elaine"—Mom squinted at her checklist—"please go get the first-aid kit from the bathroom, and let's not forget shampoo."

"Barbara is excited that she can come with us," Elaine remarked. "Her family doesn't usually attend camp meeting, so she's looking forward to it."

"Yes, I've talked with her mother and explained that we'll pick her up on our way," Mom said.

"How about the throw rugs? Are they ready too, or shall I go and get them?" questioned Elaine.

"Good girl. Yes, go get them. They're in the dryer and are ready to go," Mom said with a nod. Elaine was already running down the stairs.

When she returned, Elaine had remembered the camp meeting cantata. "Did you ever write any words to songs, Mom, as Mrs. LaTour suggested?"

"Yes, I did," Mom said.

"Well, can we see them?"

"I guess so. I was going to keep them for a surprise, but let me get them." Mom went to her suitcase and came back with a notebook. She sat down on the sofa, and the girls joined her. Handing each of them a copy of the script, she said, "Let's sing a couple of the songs together. That way you will get the idea, and then you can sing the rest while I continue to pack and get organized. This first one is set to the tune of 'O Christmas Tree.' You know these tunes, girls, so sing with enthusiasm."

> O dear Grand Ledge, O dear Grand Ledge,
> We honor you this evening.
> With shouts and cheers, with flags and tears,
> We raise our voice in singing.
> O dear Grand Ledge, we love you so,
> Each year we come and then we go,
> Back home to baths and beds, heigh-ho!
> And telephones a-ringing.

Pausing before they continued, the girls laughed.

"Oh, Mom, you're good," Elaine sighed.

"The next poem is set to 'Yankee Doodle,' that old patriotic song," Mom explained. She waved her hand in time to the music as they sang:

> To Grand Ledge we like to come
> Each summer for camp meeting;
> We meet dear friends, both old and new,
> And find the time is fleeting . . .

"Well, that's what I've done," said Mom when they'd finished the whole thing. "Do you like it?"

Both girls grinned and gave their approval. "It's great,

Mom!" exclaimed Elaine. "All the kids—and the grown-ups, too—will love it."

Marcia agreed. "You're a real poet! You make it seem so easy and simple to write poems. I'm gonna try writing poetry too when I grow up."

"You don't have to wait that long, honey," Mom said. "My mother and I wrote rhymes together when I was your age. Whenever I'd get bored, my mother would suggest we write poetry."

Then Mom went back to her packing, and the girls sang the familiar tunes together. The words to the next song were set to the tune "Oh, My Darling, Clementine."

> On the outskirts of a city called Grand Ledge
> 　　　there lies a camp
> Here we gather every summer, weather good,
> 　　　or weather damp.
> Some in tents and some in cabins, some in
> 　　　trailers by the score,
> It is one big happy family, and there's always
> 　　　room for more.
> Interesting are the meetings, we buy books ga-
> 　　　lore to read,
> Kids make crafts and go to campfires. Camp
> 　　　fulfills our every need.
> O our special, dear camp meeting, if we're
> 　　　weary or we're worn
> We will never miss a session, come high water
> 　　　or a storm.

"Boy, oh, boy!" exclaimed Marcia. "Are we ever gonna have fun with these."

⁂

When they arrived at the campground, Mom and her friends found they were all grouped together just as they'd requested. The LaTours' tent came first, then the Campbells', then the one for Elaine's family. Next were the tents of friends Minerva and Helen, who were "Detroit girls," just like Kathleen and Ruby. What a lively group those "city gals" made.

People from all over Michigan were there, and some from other states. People walking past their tent waved or stopped and talked. That's just the way it always was at camp meeting. Elaine laughed when Barbara, who was at camp meeting for the first time, said, "Your folks know everyone."

"Yeah, that's part of the fun. Thing is, when you come year after year, you get to know others who are here every year too. So you say hi to them as well as your old friends. It's a wonder we get everything unpacked and put away, there's so many people to talk to. It's exciting!"

All the kids pitched in and carried stuff from the cars. They knew this was part of their responsibility. No skipping off until the chores were done was the rule at camp meeting. Donn had brought his wagon this year, and he enthusiastically helped anyone and everyone in transporting heavy things. He grinned his appreciation when Dad slipped him a few well-deserved coins for his good-natured assistance. (Dad knew Donn's intent was to earn a bit of cash.) Of course, the men took time to laugh, joke, and visit with each other as they unloaded the cars.

"Listen to my dad laugh," chuckled Elaine to Barbara. "He could be a Santa Claus!"

The women quickly settled into their tent homes. The things that Mom brought made life as comfortable as possible. After all, she was used to camp meeting tents because she had gone every summer with her own parents when she was a girl.

With Mom's help Dad tacked the old but pretty flowered sheets to the tent's broad center frame. The sheets divided the sleeping area from the front "family room" area, making a nice privacy screen. If you wanted, you could nap in the "back room" while people visited in the "family room." Next, in the "family room" they set up a couple folding chairs, a small table, and some low shelves on one side, and an Army cot on the other side. When Dad was there, Barbara would sleep on the cot. Otherwise, she'd sleep in the back room with Mom, Elaine, and Marcia.

The tents had wooden floors, so the last thing to be done was for Dad to roll out the carpet on the "family room" floor. Then he hung a small, framed mirror on the center front tent pole so that everyone could check their hair and faces and perhaps primp a bit before they left the tent. The lawn chairs were set up outside, and before you could say "Jack Robinson," Mom and Dad had their small tent house looking spic and span. In fact, Dad announced that it looked "quite spiffy."

The man with the ice wagon came along just at the right time, and Mom bought small blocks of ice for the coolers. Then after eating the light lunch Mom fixed, Dad drove home. "See ya later," he said as he hugged his "girls."

"Let's go see if our meeting tents are in the same place," Cheryl suggested, and she, Marcia, and Arlene ran off like shots from a gun. Of course, they were familiar with the campgrounds and knew their way around very well.

"Come on, Barbara," Elaine told her, "let's go strolling to see who's here already." Sure enough, Elaine met up with several of her camp meeting pals. She introduced them to Barbara, and then they all went to see if the Book and Bible House was open. New children's books were featured every year, and they wanted to see them immediately. Then in walked Janet, a girl from their home church. Elaine and Barbara were so glad to see her. Before they could turn around, up walked Missie, the new girl. Of course, she wasn't so new anymore, but everyone was glad to see her. At least four girls from their Sabbath school class would be at camp meeting.

For supper Mom served sandwiches and veggies with dip, along with her super-good chocolate-chip cookies. Elaine, Marcia, and Barbara ate the cookies and picked up the crumbs and ate them, too. Everyone was ready in plenty of time for the first meeting, so they sat outside the tent to talk and watch the people go by. A little past 7:00 they took off to go to their meeting.

After the evening meeting the kids came home excited.

"Guess what, Mom? Elder Tony Castlebuono is in charge of our junior department. He's so good. We *love* him," Elaine bubbled, but all the kids were talking at the same time.

"Elder Castlebuono is, indeed, good," said Mom, and the other mothers she'd been visiting with fully agreed. "When he was a boy, he and his family attended the church my father pastored in Chicago," Mom reminded Elaine. "My dad and his dad were close friends."

"I think you personally introduced us to him last year or the year before," Kathleen remarked.

Ruby nodded. "It was a thrill to meet him. He is so well-liked. And to think that your father baptized his father. That's amazing."

Bill spoke up. "I hope he plans to give out free tickets for pizza the way he did last year. Remember?" All the kids nodded.

"You won't want to miss the meeting when he gives out the tickets to the kids who attend," Kathleen told her boys. "Usually it's on a Thursday, I think, and he serves the pizza on Friday at noon. I don't know if that's what he'll do this year, but I'd think so."

"Oh, there's no danger of us missing meetings," Donn said, and the others agreed.

Bill turned to his friend Buddy. "Where's Aristotle, anyway? You sure he's coming?"

"Yeah, he should be here tomorrow," Buddy replied.

"Good," said Bill. "It wouldn't be camp meeting without him."

Elaine got such a charge out of the older boys. It was kind of a social-standing thing to be friends of academy boys.

"We had some good news in our meeting, too," spoke up Arlene. "Josephine Cunnington Edwards is coming tomorrow, and she'll be here for a couple days. Everyone knows that she tells the most exciting mission stories. We're glad she's going to be here."

The talk went on as everyone drank lemonade and sat around visiting. All the kids thought that this was the very best part of camp meeting—being together with their friends.

By bedtime the girls were ready to fall in, and so was Mom. Barbara and Elaine were in one bed. Marcia and Mom were in the other. They fell asleep quickly, listening to the gentle flapping of the tent.

Bright and early the next morning Mom got up and went to the bathhouse to take a shower. The girls heard her laughing as she came back with Kathleen.

"You scoundrel, you!" Mom was saying. "If I hadn't already been awake, you surely would have done a good job with that cold water."

She opened the tent flap and came in, and Elaine and Marcia jumped up to see what all the excitement was about.

"I was taking a nice warm shower in one stall, and Kathleen was in the one next to me," Mom explained.

"All of a sudden Kathleen threw a pitcher of cold water over the top of the stall, and it drenched me."

The girls burst into giggles. "What?" they chorused. "*Cold* water?"

"Icy cold," Mom said. "At least it felt icy." She'd gone beyond the flowered sheet curtain into the "bedroom" and was getting dressed. "Really, though, it felt kind of good. I was ready to rinse off anyway. I remember that last year she pulled that stunt on Ruby."

Elaine poked her head beyond the edge of the curtain. "We're getting off to a good start, huh, Mom," she laughed. Her eyes twinkled with amusement.

Barbara grinned too. "You have such good times here," she said. "I'm glad I came."

After breakfast when the kids had gone to their meetings and Mom and her friends were alone together, Kathleen brought up the cantata. "Did you do anything with the assignment I gave you?" she asked, her eyes sparkling with delight.

"I thought you'd never mention it," Mom teased, and she went to the shelf to get her notebook. Kathleen had asked Ruby, Minerva, and Helen to join them, so Mom gave each one a copy of the new words to the old songs. She'd brought several copies with her just for that.

It didn't take the women long to catch on to the process. They sat and sang and laughed until they could hardly catch their breath.

"This one sung to 'Clementine' is so funny," Kathleen gasped, wiping tears of laughter from her eyes.

"The 'Yankee Doodle' one is clever too," said Ruby.

"Well, I like the—" Helen began, and they all laughed.

"Truth is, my dear," Minerva told Mom, "they're all great. Everyone's going to love them."

When the kids came for lunch, Kathleen had them all sit down, gave them the sheets of paper with the words, and explained the cantata. Then she led out in the singing while the kids joined in. What a time!

"Elaine, your mom's a real pro," said Bill. Of the group, he was the best musician of them all. "I'm gonna get Buddy. He'll enjoy this. He loves music too." And without looking back Bill ran off to search for his friend.

A minute or two later he returned and found the group singing yet another of the songs, so Bill and Buddy joined in singing to the tune of "Old MacDonald."

> Michigan, it has a camp, E-I-E-I-O.
> And on this camp we have some tents, E-I-E-I-O.
> With a flap, flap here, and a flap, flap there,
> Here a squeak, there a leak, everywhere a
>   creak, creak,
> Michigan, it has a camp, E-I-E-I-O!

The kids just belted out E-I-E-I-O, clapping in time to the music.

"We've got to show this to the conference president,

don't you agree?" Minerva looked at each of her friends.

Helen nodded vigorously. "I'll go find him and give him this copy right away."

"Don't you dare," exclaimed Mom. "I don't want to be 'shunned,' as the Quakers do to those members they disown. I did this just for us, no one else."

All the dads were there on the first Sabbath of camp meeting. Each family in Mom's group of friends contributed two or three dishes of food, and they put it all together in a potluck. Ruby was a trained dietitian, and she came up with interesting, delicious dishes. How the kids could eat! Maybe playing hard outside made them extra hungry.

That afternoon, at the meeting in the large pavilion, Bill played a clarinet solo. All his friends went to hear him. He was an excellent musician and played beautifully, and had been asked to be on this program for the past few years. His mother, Kathleen, was an accomplished musician herself, and so she accompanied him on the piano.

Barbara, Janet, and Missie told Elaine they were glad they'd gotten to know Bill, thanks to her. "He's really nice, and cute, too," they said.

And listening to Bill play his clarinet and hearing all the other great camp meeting music got Elaine to thinking. "Mom," she asked, "when we get home, may I take piano lessons? I really want to."

Mom was happy to hear the question. "That's a great

idea," she said. "I'll talk with Dad, and I'm sure he'll agree. One of the schoolteachers, Mrs. Greer, teaches piano. We'll look into it." Mom was delighted that Elaine wanted to learn to play the piano.

And that's how Elaine began her journey with music. After camp meeting, all arrangements were made.

SIX

A Storm, and Waving at a Bigwig

Each day of camp meeting week was filled with adventures for the kids. They made crafts and projects, took nature walks, watched the gymnastic shows put on by college students, and, of course, attended the fun evening campfires—almost everyone's favorite time.

One evening at campfire, one of the college boys who helped the leader with the programs stood up and said, "I've been asked to keep you entertained until our special musicians arrive. They're here on the campground, so they should be arriving any minute."

"Tell us a story," shouted one kid.

"No. Tell us a joke," yelled another boy. (It sounded like Donn to Elaine.)

The college guy looked around a bit helplessly, and then his face brightened with an idea. He hunched his shoulders, leaned forward, squinted his eyes, and with a look of suspicion began to speak. His words were low, slow, and deliberate—filled with apprehension and anxiety.

"The night was dark. We sat around the campfire. The captain said, 'Sir Anthony, tell us a story . . .'"

The kids leaned forward. They were about to hear

something strange and terrifying, and they were all ears. Leaves rustled. Somewhere in the darkness a twig snapped. The juniors strained to hear what came next. And the storyteller leaned toward his audience, saying in a deep, mysterious voice, "The night was dark. We sat around the campfire. The captain said, 'Sir Anthony, tell us a story . . .'"

Elaine looked at Missie, who was sitting next to her. Missie looked back and shrugged. They were puzzled, but the voice continued, still puzzling and mystifying: "The night was dark. We sat around the campfire. The captain said, 'Sir Anthony, tell us a story . . .'"

A kid's voice called out, "Hurry up, or we'll be here all night!"

The campers laughed and yelled out their agreement. "Yeah. Get on with it!"

Just then the musicians arrived with their instruments. The college guy grinned at the crowd and took a bow. His performance was met with surprised—but happy—applause. What a great job he'd done, keeping them entertained. He'd had no story to tell them, but he'd held them spellbound and kept them interested, even if the story amounted to nothing.

What a night the kids had singing, then listening to Elder Castlebuono's stories. They went skipping back to their tents singing a lively song with enthusiasm.

"'The night was dark. We sat around the campfire . . .'" was heard around the camp for several days. And every time someone said it, the others laughed.

The mothers were puzzled when Marcia, Cheryl, and Arlene asked for more extra plastic spoons, but they didn't give it too much thought. They figured the girls wanted them for the food tent. Who knew? It certainly was nothing important.

Little did the mothers know that Cheryl had come up with a secret idea, and for all Marcia and Arlene knew, Cheryl may have gotten it from her brother Donn. At any rate, it was an exciting scheme. Cheryl explained that it was possible to hide behind the thicket of bushes that lined the outer walls of the big pavilion. She led the way into the large hedge ambush.

"Now," she whispered, "let's squish ourselves down so no one can see us."

It took some effort to part the branches, squat down, and pull the bushes in around them, but at last they made themselves quite inconspicuous.

"Now, then," Cheryl whispered, "pick off some of the small, hard buds from the branches." The girls followed their leader's instructions.

"OK, here's what you do," Cheryl told them. Then using her plastic spoon as a catapult, she shot a hard bud "bullet" into the air. It sailed beyond the bushes and into the walkway on the other side. "Now you try," she told them.

Stifling their giggles, they both tried, and after two or three shots, they did pretty well.

"That's good," she said. Her lips barely moved. "Got the hang of it?"

Marcia and Arlene nodded.

"OK. Be ready."

Soon a camp guard walked by. Cheryl was the first to fire her missile. The man just brushed at his shoulder, apparently giving little thought to what may have touched him, and kept on walking.

Looking at each other with wide eyes, the girls were inspired. Young or old, and especially the camp guards— all were attacked with the bud bullets. The hits never made much of an impression on any of the people who were shot. Still, it's a wonder the girls didn't get caught. Of course, there was the possibility that no one even felt the small buds hitting their backs. The girls didn't reckon with that. But more likely, those who felt the nip of a bud on their back thought it had fallen from a tree—if they thought about it at all.

One of the guards did stop and look up in the tree above him. (Marcia fired the shot that hit his back.) Watching with grins that split their faces, the girls nodded at each other. They dared not say a word. When he walked on, Cheryl whispered, "He probably thought something had fallen on him from those giant trees."

"Yeah. He probably thought a squirrel had dropped a nut," Arlene giggled.

"Shhhhhh," the others gasped.

"Who said girls can't be soldiers?" Arlene asked later after they'd worked their way out of the underbrush.

Their arms and hands were decorated with small scratches and cuts from the prickly thicket branches, but they thought the scratches were well worth it.

"Girls will be girls, just like boys will be boys, right?" asked Marcia, and they laughed together about their secret war attack.

❦

Almost every day the kids went to the food tent. The food tent was especially fun because it was there they could taste any and all the samples of new foods that were for sale in the campus store.

"Yuck, this one's sorta awful," Elaine said with a puckered face one afternoon. It was a kind of spread on a cracker.

"Try this one," said Barbara. "It's not bad." She pointed Elaine toward an electric skillet with some kind of burger.

Round and round they went. Everyone had an opinion.

"I don't like this herbal tea. It's strange."

"Yeah. Tastes like medicine."

"Here's a good banana bread."

"Now, *this* oatmeal cookie tastes great!"

That evening they shared another potluck suppertime. The women put together the food they'd prepared, then cleaned up and sat to visit and just relax. Before going to their evening meetings, they sang a few cantata songs. By now the kids' favorite was the one sung to the tune of

"Old MacDonald." How they'd laugh as they belted out the words:

> With a flap, flap here, and a flap, flap there,
> Here a squeak, there a leak, everywhere a
>   creak, creak,
> Mich-i-gan, it has a camp, E-I-E-I-O!

The words "squeak," "leak," and "creak" took on new meaning when the weather turned miserable one night. Rain pelted the tents, and thunder rumbled in the distance. In the middle of the night Mom woke up, awakened by the sound and feel of a furious wind. The canvas tent flapped loudly.

"Mom," whispered Elaine, "what's happening?"

"It's a summer storm," she answered. "Stay covered. Everything's OK so far."

But just as the night began to dim and the faintest light grayed the darkness, the storm increased in strength. And before they knew what was happening, a gust of roaring, wild wind hit their tent, and it all but collapsed. The top of the tent dropped down almost on their heads—but not quite. A small box fell from the center shelf and hit Elaine on the head, but it didn't injure her. It just scared the wits out of her.

"Mom! Oh, Mom!" the girls yelled.

"Stay in bed, girls. At least we're dry and have cover over our heads. I'll get some help."

Mom grabbed her raincoat and crawled out of the tent. Kathleen and Ruby were already scurrying toward her.

"Are you OK, Ruth? Are the girls all right?" were their first questions.

"We're not hurt, but isn't this a mess!"

And then suddenly the wind died down, the rain stopped, and the clouds began to thin and blow away. Looking up at the sky, the women began to laugh. They just couldn't stop. Ruby's husband, Cal, who was taking his vacation at camp meeting, had gone for help. Before long they saw him running back to the disaster site followed by three camp workers.

As soon as it was determined that neither Mom nor the girls were injured, the workers steadied the poles and had the tent back up in no time flat. Miraculously, the canvas had not been ripped, so no repairs had to be made to the tent. Now they stood outside in the clothes they'd quickly thrown on. No one's hair was combed or anything, but Kathleen got out her camera.

"Look pathetic now," she said, and everyone again roared with laughter. But there was no need to tell Mom and the girls to *try* to look pathetic—they truly *did*!

Others on the campground were not as fortunate. The tents of some had been torn, letting rain pour in on beds and clothes and food. Some of those people packed up and left. Others moved into some empty tents. No lives were lost, and there were no serious injuries, but what a time they'd had! That evening the main auditorium was filled with songs of thankfulness and praise.

Dad learned about the storm when he arrived for the weekend. He sat with Frank and the other husbands, listening to the woeful tale. Of course, the kids had to include their own versions of what had happened, and everyone had a good laugh.

Donn and Bill began singing, "With a flap, flap here, and a creak, creak there," grinning as they sang.

"You're laughing at our expense," Elaine protested, giving them a poke, but she laughed as heartedly as the others did.

Elaine and Marcia will long remember that camp meeting storm.

Immediately after camp meeting Elaine began studying piano, and she loved it. Mom hardly ever had to remind her to practice. It was something she undertook with enjoyment. She was well acquainted with her teacher, Mrs. Greer, who taught at the church school. Elaine liked the way she would explain the style of music and how it should be played. Marcia listened with interest off and on during the practice sessions. In her young heart she too began to love music, and when she asked if she could take lessons, she was told she could. So now there were two budding pianists in the family.

"Today is July 4, girls, so guess what?" Mom's eyes sparkled with merriment.

"I know," replied Elaine immediately. "We're going to the parade! Right?"

"Absotively! Positootly!" Dad said with a grin.

Just then the phone rang, and Dad answered. The girls could tell by the good-natured, one-sided conversation that he was talking to a friend. "Yeah . . . That sounds great . . . OK, we'll plan on being there," Dad replied before he hung up. "That was Don Cole. Tonight we'll meet up with their family at the Pearl Street Bridge over the Grand River to watch the fireworks."

"Great!" said both Elaine and Marcia. "That sounds like fun." The Cole kids—Brent, Denise, and Suzie—were fun friends. The two families often took picnic lunches and visited the zoo together on Sabbath afternoons.

"Well, it will be fun to go to the fireworks tonight," Mom said. "But now make sure your beds are made, and then you can play outside. It's not time yet to go to the parade."

The girls scampered off.

❧❀❧

Dad knew it wouldn't be easy to find a parking space for the parade, so he had his "girls" get in the car early, and they all headed for downtown. Suddenly he pointed ahead. "Look, here's a good spot. Just made for us. We won't have far to walk, either." He quickly pulled into the space. The car just fit.

"Good for you, honey," said Mom. "Somehow you always seem to find just the right site."

Everyone got out. Dad locked the car, and they began walking to find a place to stand where they could get a good view of all the attractions. They made their way through the crowd that was already gathering early, and then they found a spot where the girls could stand in front right on the curbing. It was ideal.

People lined both sides of the street, and everyone was in a good mood. Smiles came readily and easily. It didn't seem long at all to Elaine before she could hear band music in the distance. Then the color guard came into view.

Elaine poked Marcia. "Watch for the drum majors. They'll be twirling batons and throwing them up in the air." Both girls were excited, and so were the kids standing next to them.

Sure enough, the parade began with the color guards coming first, and then the drum majors, followed by a military band. Wow, could they play! Next came a small group of city officials, and people around them started cheering and shouting, "Hi, Jerry!" A friendly-looking man in a black suit smiled and waved to the lively crowd on either side of the avenue. Elaine was puzzled, and she turned to her dad with a questioning look on her face.

Dad leaned over and said, "That's Gerald Ford, our Grand Rapids congressman. He works in Washington, D.C."

"Wow!" Elaine exclaimed. She understood that this man was an important figure, although she'd never seen or heard of him before. He did have a nice smile, and he waved energetically.

"Does he live near the president?" Marcia asked excitedly, and Dad nodded.

"He's a bigwig," Elaine whispered in her sister's ear.

There were more bands, school kids, floats carrying pretty girls, and clowns. The fire truck blew its mournful siren, and the firefighters threw pieces of wrapped candy to the kids. Elaine and Marcia ran and grabbed as many pieces as they could. What fun! The float carrying Winnie the Pooh was cheered for loudly and strongly by the children in the crowd. Another float featured Davy Crockett.

All the players in the bands were dressed smartly, and they kept perfect step. "How do they play and march at the same time without losing their place in the music?" Elaine asked Marcia. A nod of Marcia's head told Elaine that she wondered the same thing.

When the parade ended, Dad suggested they each have an ice-cream cone from the man who had his ice-cream stand nearby. Mom, of course, got chocolate. Dad got his usual vanilla, and the girls asked for their cones to be dipped and sprinkled with delicious tiny bits of candy.

Some years later, when Dad was president of his local Rotary club, he invited Representative Ford to come and be a guest speaker for a club meeting. Sure enough, he came, and Dad had his picture taken shaking hands with him. Little did any of them know—including Representative Ford—that someday that man would become the thirty-eighth president of the United States.

SEVEN

Tornado

"Let's ride our bikes down to the corner variety store and get something," Cindy suggested one morning.

"OK. Sounds great," Elaine replied. "I'll tell my mom where we're goin', and then I'll be right out."

"Don't hurry yourself," Cindy said with a grin. "Remember, we're on vacation. I'll go swing with Marcia while I wait. I see she's out there."

Elaine went into the house, spoke to her Mom, and grabbed a dime from the little change purse in her dresser drawer. She knew it wouldn't buy very much, but it would do. Then she ran to the backyard.

Marcia was sitting on the double horsey swing, and Elaine plopped herself down in the swing next to Cindy.

"What a great day," Cindy yawned. "Just look at those fluffy clouds."

"They really are big ones," agreed Elaine. "Huge cotton balls is what they are."

"They'd make good pillows," Marcia said, and the three girls chuckled.

Kerry came running through the gate. "Hi, Marcia! Hi, everyone! Can I join ya?"

"Sure," called Marcia. Elaine and Cindy said, "Hi and 'bye," then pedaled away.

❧

The store owners, Mr. and Mrs. Morgan, were a friendly couple, and the neighborhood folks respected them. "Howdy, gals," Harley Morgan called with a big smile. He was putting boxes of merchandise on the shelves.

Mrs. Morgan greeted them too. She worked as the cashier. "Take your time and look around, girls," she said with a friendly grin.

While Elaine had not been in the store often, she was somewhat familiar with the layout. The girls walked past the magazine rack, the pharmaceuticals and cosmetics, and the coffee machine and sandwiches until they came to the "goodies" section. There they tried to decide which treat they wanted.

Working over against the wall as he stocked shelves with cans of automotive oils was Davy, the friend of Cindy's brother Jeff. Elaine had seen him several times at Cindy's. He turned and spoke to the girls too.

"Hi, Davy," Cindy said. She took Elaine's hand, and they walked over to him. Davy stood on a short ladder arranging things on the upper shelves. "Hi again," he said. He smiled down on the girls, and they talked a bit.

"Hey, Cindy," he said, as if he'd just remembered to tell her. "My sister, Mandy, has just been accepted at Calvin College beginning this fall term. She thinks she wants to study nursing, and she's really excited."

"Wow! That's good news. I can't wait to tell LuAnn the next time we talk on the phone," Cindy said. "She'll be excited too."

He is so nice, and cute, too. Someday when I have a boyfriend, I want him to be like Davy or Jeff or Bill or Buddy, thought Elaine, but she kept the thought to herself.

The girls went back to do their shopping and roaming and chatting. As they passed the greeting cards, Cindy stopped and said, "My mom says this is kinda like the five and dime store she used to go to when she was young. She told us that in those stores you could buy lots of different things, such as greeting cards, needles and thread, brooms, makeup, and things for the house. Sometimes they even sold inexpensive jewelry and clothes, too."

"Seems like I've heard my mom mention dime stores too," Elaine replied.

Mrs. Morgan overheard the conversation. She walked toward the girls. "I'm old enough to remember those olden days too, girls," she said with a chuckle. "We lived in Chicago when I was growing up, and the big dime stores there were Kresge's and Woolworth's. They weren't nearly as big as Marshall Field's or Carson Pirie Scott's department stores, but their big, curved showcase windows were always filled with things I longed to have. We kids liked walking around in the store just to look at stuff. The first and only teddy bear I ever had came from Woolworth's. I named him Woolie. Wasn't that a cute name?"

The girls nodded. It *was* a cute name. Cindy called after Mrs. Morgan with a question. "Mrs. Morgan, everything in those dime stores didn't cost a dime," she asked. "Did they?"

"No, they didn't. That would have been good for the customers, but not for the owners," she said. "Maybe when they first opened, most things were a dime, but not when I shopped there." She turned to walk back to the front of the store, then stopped. "That's a good question. I wonder why they were called 'dime stores' when lots of things cost a dollar or more." She was shaking her head as she walked on.

"I'm gonna get some bubble gum with my money," Cindy announced.

"Well, I think I'm gonna get this bag of M&M's," Elaine replied. So they made their purchases, thanked Mrs. Morgan, and then left the store, chewing and laughing.

"Did I ever tell you about that fellow Davy?" Cindy asked as they pedaled toward home.

"Don't think so. What about him? He seems nice whenever we meet."

"Oh, he's a nice guy, that's for sure. Our family has known his for a long time, even before the accident."

"They had an accident?" Elaine asked as they pedaled along.

"Yeah. A bad one. I was so little that I don't much remember it, but I've heard about it many times."

"Well, tell me. I'm all ears." Elaine threw a couple M&M's into her mouth. "I see him with your brother a lot."

"Yeah, Jeff and Davy are great pals. Davy was voted sergeant at arms of his high school class for a couple of years now. Jeff teases him that he has memorized *Robert's Rules of Order* just so he can boss everyone around. But he's only teasing Davy."

"What's *Robert's Rules of Order,* anyway?" Elaine asked.

"It's a book that gives instructions on how to conduct meetings properly," Cindy explained.

"What about the accident?" asked Elaine.

"Oh, yeah, I almost forgot. Well, when Davy was in grade school—I'm too young to remember when this all happened—but he and his sister were riding in the car with their dad when they had an awful accident. Their dad was killed, and his sister was badly injured. Davy was the lucky one. He had a broken arm, but that was all." She screwed up her face, thinking. "I seem to remember that their dad had made a wrong turn, so the police said the accident was his fault. They never had had a lot of money anyway, and now there were lots of financial problems for the family."

"But their dad was dead. How could it be his fault?"

"I don't know. Whatever it was, it kept the family from getting insurance money or something like that."

The two rode along in silence until Elaine said, "Poor Davy. What happened to his sister?"

"Mandy had lots of injuries. I don't remember what all, but she was in the hospital a long time. When she first came home, she had to be in a wheelchair. She's OK now. She got behind in school, of course, but she caught up and graduated this year with LuAnn. She does have a very slight limp, but you'd hardly notice. Everyone likes her. In fact, she's cute and quite popular. Mandy and my sister always have dates for anything big that goes on at school." Cindy nodded her head and smiled. "Of course, they both have such good personalities that it's no wonder they're popular."

"I've seen her with LuAnn," said Elaine. "Go on. You were going to tell me about Davy."

"Well, something happened to Davy after the accident. My mom said it made him bitter, losing his dad and all. He got nasty to everyone, and he wouldn't study. He'd pick fights and slug anyone who got in his way. He'd trip the girls or knock them off the swings if he could. He got black eyes from some of the older boys he'd punched in the gut. Jeff said he slunk around like a bum and acted as though he hated everyone. Mom says she thinks most parents told their kids not to fight with Davy, but he was in a heap of trouble all the time.

"I guess his teachers were sympathetic and understanding, but he was just a creep."

"Did he run around with a gang?" Elaine asked, her eyes big.

"Naw. He didn't really run around with anyone 'cause he didn't have time to. He had to go home right away after school to help out."

"He sure doesn't act nasty now," Elaine said as the girls drew up to Cindy's yard. They parked their bikes, then sat on Cindy's front porch to continue talking.

"Well, Jeff was the only one Davy was decent to. Jeff stayed friends with him, but I've heard Davy say that it didn't make a difference. He was just plain ornery. All the kids stayed out of his way. But my folks let Davy come over whenever he wanted to."

Cindy picked up a blade of grass and put it to her lips. Nope. No sound. "My dad says that it was finally Harley Morgan who made a difference in Davy's life," she continued. "Every day or two Mr. Morgan saw Davy walk around the store, just looking at things. Davy would come in, look around some, then leave. Mr. Morgan kept his eye on him, but Davy never took a thing. He just looked. Finally, one day Mr. Morgan went over and asked Davy how he was and talked to him a bit. You know how friendly he is. Well, he asked Davy if he saw something he liked.

"Davy nodded and pointed at a small comb and mirror set. 'How much is that, Mr. Morgan?' he asked, bashful-like.

"'Why do you ask, Davy? That's not a boy's toy,' Mr. Morgan told him.

"'Oh, no, sir, I know that,' Davy told him. 'I thought my sister would like it for her birthday. Don't know if I could afford it. That's what I was wonderin' is all,' he said.

"'Tell you what, Davy,' Mr. Morgan said, 'would you like to come in and help me out here in the store—maybe sweeping the floors after school? In no time you can afford to buy your sister that gift you're a-lookin' at. I'll keep track of your time. Ask your mom. See what she says.'

"Davy was all excited. 'I'll ask my mother right away. I kinda think she'll let me. We don't have lots of money, ya know, and this would be a help.'

"My dad says that Harley Morgan's befriending Davy made all the difference in the world. And that's how

Davy started working in the store. He's been there ever since. He got so he knew how to stock the shelves, and he helped Harley in lots of ways. For payment for his labor, Davy got free stuff to take home. Sometimes it was groceries, and sometimes goodies. But Dad said that working kept him occupied, and soon he was his old self again—not nasty and hateful. Now he even answers the phone, and he knows how to operate the cash register, too."

"Wow!" Elaine could hardly believe it. Not that she thought Cindy was telling her a fairy tale, but it was strange to think of Davy like that.

"Well, I'd better go in," said Cindy, standing up. "My grandma and grandpa from Escanaba are here, so Mom told me not to spend all morning with you," she laughed, "even though I'd like to."

"Where on earth is Escanaba?" Elaine asked. The name was fun to say.

"Escanaba is in the upper peninsula of Michigan, way, way up north. Grandpa's glad they built the Mackinac Bridge, because it makes their travel time much shorter. But even with the bridge it's quite a trip for them to come to our house."

"Now that I think about it, I do remember hearing about Escanaba," said Elaine. She looked up at the sky as she kicked up her bike stand and turned toward home. "Wow, the wind sure has picked up."

"Yeah, and the sun's not as bright as it was," Cindy noticed. "Wonder if there's a storm brewing."

As Elaine pedaled down the street and turned into

her driveway, she saw that Mom was taking some blankets off the clothesline. Marcia and Kerry were swinging on the swings vigorously, jumping off and on to see how far they could get each time.

"I'll take the clothes basket for you, Mom," Elaine offered when she saw that her mother had blankets folded over her arms.

"Thanks, Elaine. I think we'd better go in now." She scanned the sky. "It looks like we're going to get a pretty good rain. Kerry, you'd better run along home."

"Oh, do we have to stop right now?" Marcia asked, swinging energetically.

"We can run real fast if it rains on us," Kerry called.

"No, you better stop now," Mom said. "Kerry, your mother will want you at home." So the girls jumped off. Kerry said goodbye and skipped away.

Marcia stood at the front door and watched her little friend run across the street. The sky did get darker, but there was no thunder, so Marcia figured she could have stayed outside longer.

"I'm gonna go back and swing all by myself, Mom."

"No, Marcia, you stay indoors for now. Why not play with your Lite-Brite?"

But Marcia went back to the door and longingly looked through the screen to see if there were any other kids out there. Elaine sat down at the piano and began practicing a new piece she was learning.

Finally, a bit exasperated, Marcia called out, "Mom, it isn't raining yet. I knewdist it wouldn't."

Elaine stopped short, raising her hands from the keys. She was laughing out loud.

"What did you just say, Marcia?" asked Mom.

Marcia turned to face her mother. "I just said I knewdist it wouldn't rain. And it's not going to. What's so funny?" She understood that she may have said something not quite right, and the puzzled look on her face was mixed with a smile.

"It's the word you used. You said 'knewdist,' and a nudist is a naked person," Mom explained.

"Nudist," giggled Elaine. "Nudist. That's a great one. Wait till we tell Dad."

Marcia couldn't help laughing at herself. "You know what I mean," she said grinning from ear to ear.

"We know, honey. We know what you meant. Now, then, listen to that thunder. And look. It's begun to rain. I knewdist it would," chuckled Mom. "Let's check all the windows."

It rained, and the wind blew, and it all got worse and worse. Hard raindrops pelted the windows, and the wind made the shutters rattle.

"This is some storm!" Mom said a moment later. "I think we'd better go to the basement. I wish Dad were home."

Just then they heard the beginning of a rumbling roar. It quickly grew louder until it seemed to envelop the house. The girls ran with their mother down the basement steps. The house shook and the wind screamed—they could still hear it in the basement. Minutes passed as they listened, trembling with fear. Mom wrapped her arms around her girls and prayed aloud for their safety and for Dad, wherever he was. They all hoped that Dad wasn't out in it.

At last the terrible roaring stopped. All they could hear were their heartbeats. Mom waited another minute or two, then carefully and hesitantly climbed the steps and cracked open the door. It was still raining, but the worst was over. "That was a terrible storm, girls," she said, "but I think it's safe to come up."

It was almost impossible to see anything outside, for the rain still poured in a fury, and a waterfall of rain covered the windows. Lightning bolts were continuous, even as the rolls of thunder sounded far away.

They all sat together on the couch and looked out the bay window. "Let's pray again that Dad is OK," Mom told them, so they bowed their heads while she offered a concerned prayer to their heavenly Father that Dad would be kept from danger.

Mom tried to use the phone, but the line was dead. There was nothing to do but wait.

It must have been two hours later that they heard Dad's car come up the driveway. They all rushed to the door. He came in and hugged them tight. "I was so worried about you," he said, giving his three "girls" another squeeze. He raised his eyes toward heaven and thanked the Lord for protecting his family and their home.

"It seems a tornado plowed through the neighborhood about two blocks away from us," he said once they'd let go of him and let him talk. "It blew through the middle of that large brick Reformed church that's down the road a short ways. Both ends of the church are still standing, but the wind tore right through its middle." He shook his head. "Nothing is left—no windows, no pews, not even the organ."

"The pews?" Mom asked. "All the pews are gone?"

"Everything! It's a disaster. I saw a lot of homes that were damaged too."

"Why are you so late?" Elaine asked. "We were scared."

"I tried to get home sooner than this, but the police had all the roads blocked off. I got as far as the Keeches' house. They saw me and had me come in with them. I was lucky to get that far. Finally I went back to the car and headed for home. I hadn't gone far when, up ahead, I could see the police waving their lights. They still weren't letting people through. So I immediately turned the corner and took some back streets home. I'm lucky I got through."

"We're glad," Marcia said, and then they were all talking at once. Marcia wanted to tell him that she'd been outside swinging and that Mom had made her come in and that she had still wanted to be outside and that all of a sudden it had become really dark and the wind had started blowing. Elaine had her own story, that she'd been down at Cindy's, and if Cindy hadn't had to go in because her grandparents were visiting then, Elaine would have been at Cindy's all through the storm, and Mom said that would have been awful, for she wouldn't have known where she was or if she was OK. Then Mom told Dad that the phone lines must be down, because their phone didn't work; and then they all went into the kitchen, where Mom asked if soup and grilled cheese sandwiches sounded like a good meal to have after a storm, and they all said yes. So everyone pitched in, each one thankful that they all were unhurt. And when they bowed their heads for the blessing, Mom again thanked God for His care. 🌸

EIGHT

Getting Stitches

 It wasn't until late afternoon the next day that Mom went outside to sweep the driveway. It was a mess. It was covered with twigs, leaves, and even small branches, all left by the previous day's tornado. First she picked up the branches and put them in a plastic trash bin. Then she started sweeping the twigs and leaves. Her kitchen broom dragged over the concrete, and she had to sweep the same spot several times to get everything. She stopped and looked up at the blue, blue sky and shook her head. Wow! You'd never guess that such a sky could produce the storm they'd had the day before. "I'd better quit daydreaming, or I'm never going to finish this," she told herself. It was going to be a bigger job than she'd thought.

In her bedroom Elaine put down the *Little House* book she was reading—*On the Banks of Plum Creek*. She never could decide which book of the series she liked best, but this was one of her favorites. The section she'd just read was about Laura being caught in the raging waters of the usually calm Plum Creek. The rain they'd had yesterday surely would swell a creek, and the tornado was just too scary. She didn't like to think about it. All that time not knowing if Dad was OK still brought a funny feeling to her chest.

Putting down the book, she decided to practice her piano lesson. She loved listening to Mrs. Greer play the piano at church. She hoped she'd play as well someday, and often listened carefully to hear the expression Mrs. Greer put into her playing—the way she played some notes loud and some soft, or the way her fingers sometimes flew across the keys while other times they played slowly and stately. Elaine always paid particular attention to her style and manner.

After she'd finished practicing she felt thirsty, so she went into the kitchen to see what she could find. Of course, there was always water, but she wanted something else. Nothing in the fridge. Oh, there was frozen orange juice. Mom had said that she was going to make it up, so Elaine decided to do it for her. Then she could have some to drink too. In fact, Mom would probably like some when she came in from sweeping the driveway.

Elaine got the can opener, opened the juice can, and pried out the concentrate with a spoon. Oops, there was still some in the bottom, so holding the frosty can in one hand, she inserted the spoon again. "Oh, *oooh!*" she screamed. "Oh, that hurts! Ohhhhhh . . ."

Running, Marcia skidded into the kitchen. "What's wrong? What happened?"

Crying, Elaine held her hand out toward her sister. Blood streamed down her fingers and onto her wrist. Quickly she held her hand over the sink and turned on the faucet.

"I'll get Mom!" Marcia gasped, and flew toward the door.

"Mom! she shouted. "Elaine's hurt. She cut herself. Hurry!"

One look at her scared face told Mom more than her words. She dropped the broom and raced after Marcia into the house. In the kitchen she found Elaine leaning over the sink, her left hand under the running faucet. Her face was gray. Fearing she was about to faint, Mom grabbed her.

"Tell me what happened, honey."

"I was going to mix up some frozen orange juice, and I cut my fingers on the jagged edge of the lid," she said weakly. "It hurts."

With one arm holding Elaine, Mom reached into a drawer with the other and pulled out a worn dish towel. "Here, sweetie," she said. "Let's wrap it in this. It's old, but it's clean."

So she sat Elaine down at the kitchen table, tightly wrapping the fingers with the towel. "Can you hold some pressure against them?" she asked. "I've got to call Dad."

Dad was out on some business with Chief Henline, a neighbor who was the local chief of police, and there was no way to reach him. But Mom called the police chief's wife and quickly explained what had happened.

"I'm sorry. I don't know where they were going," the neighbor told her. "I don't have any idea. Do you want me to come over?"

Mom told her no. She said that she'd wait a few minutes and make another phone call. She thought maybe she could find him. But just then she heard a car pull into the driveway. To her surprise, it was a police car—and in it were the police chief and Dad. They'd finished their business, and he'd brought Dad home. When Mom explained what had happened, Chief Henline said, "Bring Elaine out here immediately. I'll drive all of you to the hospital."

So away they went. Even Marcia. Riding to the hospital in a black-and-white police car! Though Elaine was still scared, it was kind of exciting.

Soon they were in the emergency room with all its hustle and bustle of nurses, doctors, and patients. And before long a nurse took Elaine and her parents and Marcia into an examining room to wait for the doctor. Elaine wrinkled her nose. "Hospitals smell funny, don't they?" she said. "I think they smell like medicine. And what are all those strange noises?"

Dad laughed. "I don't know about the noises. You can ask the doctor when he comes."

Elaine sat on the examining table, her feet swinging above the floor. She still held her hurt hand away from her body, but the nurse had replaced the bloodied dish towel with a thick square of gauze that Elaine held against the cuts. The wounds had mostly stopped bleeding, but they still hurt.

Just then a white-coated man strode into the room. A stethoscope hung around his neck, and he held a clipboard in one hand. "Elaine! What do we have here?" he exclaimed, and she looked up in happy surprise. It was none other than Dr. Ross, her friend Missie's dad. Wow! It was nice to see a familiar face. "What happened?" he asked her.

So Elaine told the story again. First, she'd told Marcia. Then she'd told Mom, then Dad and Chief Henline. And every time she told how she'd cut her fingers, it got a little less scary to her. Dr. Ross took her hand in his and carefully looked at the cuts. "These are going to require some stitches," he said, looking from Elaine to her parents. She sucked in her breath at that.

"Don't worry," he comforted. "I'm going to deaden your fingers, and you won't feel a thing."

Elaine wasn't convinced, and her mouth twisted with concern.

"You *will* feel a couple of pricks when I put in the medicine that deadens your fingers," he said, "but I'll be as gentle as possible." He sat down on a stool and looked into her eyes. "Will that be OK with you?"

"It's OK," she said in a small voice.

Dr. Ross stepped out of the room to get some supplies. When he returned, Mom and Dad and Marcia told Elaine goodbye. They'd wait outside in the ER waiting room. Elaine's lip trembled a bit as she watched them go.

A nurse came into the room and rolled a narrow tray up to the examining table where Elaine sat. "Just lie down, honey, and rest your arm on this platform," the nurse told her.

Dr. Ross slipped on a pair of very thin rubber gloves, then picked up a needle. "This is the numbing medicine," he told her. "It will feel like a beesting." She sucked in her breath again. "Have you ever been stung by a bee?" he asked, but he didn't wait for her to answer. "I have, let me tell you. I was a little kid, and I was poking around a wasps' hive. Made the wasps mad. Those wasps came buzzing out, and one zoomed right up to my arm. Before I knew it he'd gotten me good. I went crying into the house to show my mom. And you know what?" he asked Elaine.

"What?" she asked, fascinated by his story.

"After my mom fixed me up, I went back outside and poked that wasps' nest again." He laughed at his own foolishness. "I certainly got what I deserved! Got myself stung again."

Elaine laughed too.

"Did that hurt?" he asked.

She looked up, surprised. "Are you done?"

"I am with the deadening medicine. Now we'll just let it take effect, and I'll put in those stitches."

Some time later Elaine's parents were brought back into the ER. "I put two stitches in each finger," Dr. Ross told them. "She cut a tendon in one finger and did damage to muscles in both. I had to do a little exploring to find the tendon, but all will be well, I'm sure."

"Thanks so much, Dr. Don," Dad said, placing his arm around his friend's shoulders, and Mom shook his hand. "You're great; you know that, don't you?" she said, a bit teary-eyed.

"I don't know about that," he said with a laugh. "I'm just glad I was here to take care of Elaine. And talk about great. She was a real trooper."

A grateful family rode home with Marcia cuddled next to Elaine in the back seat of the chief's car. "I'm glad you're better," Marcia whispered, looking at the bandages on Elaine's fingers. "I was scared."

"Me too," Elaine whispered back.

She got along fine with her bandaged hand. She was glad it wasn't her right hand, for then she'd have had trouble writing and maybe even eating. One thing did worry her, though. She loved playing the piano, and Dr. Ross had said that she'd injured muscles in both fingers. She worried that she wouldn't be able to play the piano anymore.

"I'd think you could still play the piano," Mom told her. "Dr. Ross said that your fingers will heal fine. But why don't we ask your piano teacher?"

"Good!" Elaine agreed.

Sure enough, Mrs. Greer told her that practicing the piano once the stitches were removed would provide good exercise. "You'll strengthen your fingers, and that's what you want. They've been weakened by the injury."

"What a relief," Elaine sighed. "I don't want fingers that can't move well." And sure enough, after the stitches came out Elaine went right to the piano. Those two fingers *were* weaker, but a little practice brought them back to normal. She was so glad.

Elaine needn't have worried about her fingers. They grew strong again, and she continued practicing the piano. She did so well that when she was in high school at Andrews Academy she played the piano accompaniment for the school's outstanding choral group, the Silhouettes. Her cousin Roger sang in the baritone section, and they enjoyed being together. ❀

NINE

Elaine Saves a Life

"*Well,*" *announced Dad* one evening as he came home from work, "our trip to Colorado is coming up soon. Better start packing!"

"I've thought about that," Mom replied. "We won't be gone that long, so we don't have to take too much stuff. But I'll get things ready."

Dad untied his tie and pulled it off. "I've talked to Don Ham, and he knows when to expect us. It'll work out for him timewise, and he's as excited about seeing me as I am about seeing him." Elaine glanced up just then. Dad's face shone, and she realized that he was as excited about seeing Don as she would be to see a special friend she hadn't seen in a long time.

Elaine and Marcia worked with Mom to get everything packed and ready to go, and they drove off the following Sunday morning. It was exciting to get up early, dress quickly, and get in the car—and go. They played guessing games and counting games to help the time pass quickly, and it didn't seem long until they stopped where Dad would have a two-day seminar. The two days passed, and they were on their way to Don and Judy Ham's place. As soon as they arrived, Elaine caught the excitement.

All Dad and Don could do was laugh and talk and slap each other on the back and reminisce about their long-ago escapades in Davenport. Of course, Judy joined in. She'd grown up with them, so she knew of their romps and pranks. However, she and Mom found plenty to talk about, leaving the guys to themselves.

But it was there that Elaine and Marcia had the surprise of their lives. Don and Judy's poodle had had six puppies. Two had already been given away, but four small ones still ran and crouched and nipped and played around the house.

"Aren't they cute!" Elaine exclaimed as she held a white puffy ball of fluff in her lap. "Oh, this one is so lively. Just look how it rolls around."

All the grown-ups could see that the girls were in love with the puppies.

"Better get yourself one, Gene," said Don. "The dogs aren't miniatures, but neither are they the full-sized poodles. I would think one of these puppies would have a wonderful time in that fenced-in backyard of yours that you told me about."

Could it be that we're finally going to get a dog? Elaine wondered. *Yippee!*

By the next day one puppy in particular held their attention. It seemed the cutest and the smartest and the friendliest of the four. Elaine and Marcia lost their hearts to it.

"Get us this one, pleeeease, Dad," the girls begged.

"Well, I don't know . . ." he teased.

"Look how cute he is."

"See how smart he is."

"Well, I don't –"

"Pleeeease," they begged, and Dad grinned.

"Well, OK."

"They're all paper-trained already," Judy explained.

"That's good," Mom said with relief.

After breakfast the next morning, when the family drove off and waved goodbye, a little white poodle sat in the middle of the backseat. The sisters finally had their own dog! They were so excited they could hardly stand it. "What shall we name him?" was Elaine's first question.

"I understand that poodles were originally German hunting dogs," said Dad.

"Well, a lot of poodles are given a French name," Mom said. "Why not give ours a German name instead?"

Dad laughed. "How does Adolf sound?"

"That sounds awful," Mom laughed, punching her husband in the ribs.

"OK, how about Fritz?" was Dad's next try.

"I like that," Elaine said.

"So do I," said Marcia. "Fritzie sounds cute."

And Fritzie he became.

When Elaine and Marcia got home, they invited all the neighbor kids to come to their house and meet the new pet on the block.

And it turned out that Fritz was a very smart dog. Mom put a nice soft blanket for him in the back hall, and he adapted quickly to his new home and his own bed. He immediately settled in and loved to romp and play with the girls. He also quickly learned the rules that went with his new home. And it didn't take him long to understand that when Dad got up from his rocking chair after the late-night news and said, "Well, it's time for bed," it was time for Fritz to walk to the back hall and go to bed him-self—automatically.

❧

"Mom," Elaine called one day as she came through the door with Marcia right behind her. "Sandy invited Marcia to swim in her pool this afternoon, and she said I could come, too. May we go?"

Sandy was the little girl who lived down the street, and her family had a real inground swimming pool in their backyard.

"Please, may we go, Mom?" implored Marcia. "Sandy said that her dad is home today, so he'll be watching us."

Mom thought about it for a minute while the girls stood quietly, begging her with their eyes. Then with some reluc-tance, Mom said they could go for a half hour. Elaine was already a strong swimmer, so Mom felt comfortable allow-ing her to go to Sandy's pool. But Marcia knew only how to dog-paddle a bit. Mom had signed her up for swimming lessons at Grandville High School, beginning that very next week. So Mom decided it would be OK.

"Be careful now," Mom cautioned. "Marcia, don't go into the deep water." Excitedly the girls put on their swimsuits, grabbed some towels, and were out the door, running as fast as their legs would carry them.

"Let's see," said Mom to herself. "We're out of milk for supper, and if I quickly run to the Meijer store, I can get a few groceries and be back before the girls get home." Still feeling a bit uneasy, she drove the car out of the driveway. She had never before left the girls alone, and now she was leaving without telling them where she was going or when she would be back. She continued to argue with herself as she drove down the street and turned onto the main road to the store. She didn't feel good about it, but told herself there wasn't a problem. Both Elaine and Marcia were responsible and obedient. And she'd be back home before they returned from the pool. Meanwhile, a group of kids—Elaine, Marcia, Cindy, Kerry, Scott, and Rusty—were all in the pool having a delightful time.

Rusty had discovered how much fun it was to leap from the pool's edge with a big splash that covered the others' heads with water. Soon they made a game of it, competing to see who could make the biggest splash. While the others jumped and splashed, Cindy and Elaine raced each other from one side to the other, laughing when their race ended in a tie. Marcia and Kerry held hands and jumped. They practiced their version of swimming, and as the minutes flew by, everyone was having a wonderful time.

After a bit Marcia saw an inflatable ring that no one was using, so she grabbed it, slipped it around her waist, and jumped into the deep end. The ring held her up, and she leaned forward and began paddling around.

Elaine saw her jump and looked at her several times, a

little concerned that her sister was in water over her head. But she seemed to be doing all right, so Elaine turned back to Cindy, and they kept on playing and swimming.

The next time Elaine looked for her sister she saw that Marcia was in serious trouble. The ring had slipped away, and Marcia was frantically splashing her arms. Once she went completely under the water. When she bobbed up, her hair streamed over her face and she looked as though she was crying. Her arms splashed and her feet kicked, but that didn't help her at all.

Elaine went into action. Instead of getting out of the pool and running to the deep end to jump in, Elaine dove under the water and began to swim to the rescue from where she was. Had she not been a strong swimmer, she couldn't have made it. When she reached her sister, from underwater she gave Marcia a big shove upward and toward the edge of the pool. She shoved as hard as she could, and did this two or three times before she came up for air herself.

Then, unable to hold her breath any longer, Elaine came to the surface. She felt sure that by now Marcia would be safely at the pool's edge, but she wasn't. An inflatable raft floated between Marcia and the pool's edge. She was bobbing and splashing and reaching as far as she could, but try as she might, Marcia couldn't reach across the raft to grab the edge of the pool. She just could not make it.

In desperation Elaine shouted, "Help!" At that, Sandy's dad put down the newspaper he was reading, jumped up, and pulled first Marcia, then Elaine, out of the pool.

"Now there ya are," he said to them. "Just go ahead and play some more, but don't tell your mom about this." They looked at him soberly. He was serious. They could tell. He settled down in his chair and continued reading.

But the girls weren't interested in playing anymore. They grabbed their towels, slipped their feet into their rubber thongs, and ran home as fast as they could. They arrived just ahead of their mother. When Mom walked in a minute or two later, to her surprise she found Elaine and Marcia standing in the kitchen, their towels wrapped around their middles. Fritzie stood as close as he could to the girls, sniffing and occasionally giving their toes a little lick. With eyes as big as saucers the girls were exchanging sly glances. Puzzled, Mom asked, "What happened? Have you finished swimming already? It hasn't been a half hour since you left."

Again, Elaine and Marcia looked at each other, and Mom could tell something was bothering them. "Well," Elaine began hesitantly, "Sandy's dad said not to tell you, but we decided we would."

Then between the two of them, the whole story unfolded. Both girls were scared and exhausted.

Suddenly Mom's knees became weak. Sitting down and trying to picture the whole ordeal, she hugged the girls and said to Elaine, "You saved your sister's life. Do you realize that?"

Elaine wasn't sure she had done anything brave, but Marcia agreed that she had. "I wasn't really scared," explained Marcia, "because I knew Elaine would help me." She gave her sister a grateful smile.

"Always respect the water, girls. Don't ever think you are stronger than it is," warned Mom. "I'm sure you both learned a frightening but valuable lesson today."

That night the girls told their father all about the episode, and as they sat down to supper Dad thanked the good Lord for Elaine's quick action and bravery.

"You know," Dad said thoughtfully, "we'll never know until we reach heaven how many times angels divinely intervene in our lives and save us from a multitude of dangers. I firmly believe that. A great tragedy was avoided today. Elaine, with the assistance of an angel, you were, indeed, a lifesaver!"

The girls never went back to that neighbor's pool again, and the very next week Marcia began swimming lessons. She just loved the water, much to Mom's relief. Mom had wondered if her near-drowning might have made Marcia frightened of the water. But she learned to swim with ease and looked like a little fish darting here and there. She was the best girl swimmer in the class.

After that, Mom often took the girls swimming. Dad had joined a nearby country club that had a great golf course and a huge, lovely swimming pool. Both Elaine and Marcia became very good swimmers by practicing there.

In fact, just for fun they would reenact the "drowning," much to Mom's horror. Marcia would splash, gurgle, and gasp, "Glub, glub."

Then Elaine would pull her to a corner of the pool.

They'd laugh together. The other kids around them didn't know what they were doing, so they paid no attention to them. But that shenanigan came to an end the day the lifeguard saw them and, thinking they were in trouble, almost jumped into the water to offer assistance.

"We were just playing," Elaine explained.

"Yeah," said Marcia. "I wasn't actually in trouble."

"Well, I don't want to see you girls doing that again, *not ever*! You had me frightened," she reprimanded seriously. "Don't do that again!"

Never for a moment did the girls ever forget that water could be a deadly enemy as well as a refreshing friend. Many years later Marcia became a water safety instructor, thanks to her sister Elaine, the courageous girl who had saved her life.

TEN

Joanie James Monica

When school started in the fall, Elaine and Marcia were eager to get going. The one-story red-brick building that housed the junior academy was clean and sturdy, and it had a nice, large playground.

On the first day of school they met Mrs. Ross in the hall with Missie and John. Missie and Elaine were in the same classroom. Mom and Mrs. Ross talked with the principal and introduced him to their children. He shook hands with each of them. School was about to begin. "I'll come back to talk with both of you ladies in just a minute," he said to Mom and Mrs. Ross. He then took the two girls to their new classroom, where he introduced them to their teacher. John, Missie's brother, was in a higher grade, so he hurried to his classroom, accompanied by some of the older boys.

When the principal walked Marcia into Miss Barbara Bassham's classroom, Marcia was delighted to see that it was brightly decorated with big photos of different animals tacked to the walls. A large picture of George Washington hung over Miss Bassham's desk, and a flag stood in the corner of the room. Before classes began Miss Bassham introduced Marcia to her classmates.

Miss Carol Crider was Elaine's and Missie's teacher. Their classroom faced the front of the school building, and windows ran along one side of the room, letting in the bright sunshine. Next to the flag stood a large book cabinet. It immediately caught Elaine's attention. She sure hoped to get a chance to examine its contents and read the titles of the books real soon. Surely there would be some books she'd want to read. At first glance she saw the covers of the *Little House* books. Those were some of her favorites, and she was sure there'd be others.

Miss Crider greeted Elaine and Missie and officially introduced them to the other students. "I understand that most of you know Elaine and Missie already, but let's give them a big hand of applause to welcome them."

After the applause and the nods, Miss Crider asked the students to bow their heads. She offered a prayer that the good Lord would guide them throughout the school year. Elaine felt comfortable immediately and not the least bit self-conscious or timid.

During recess the girls had time to visit a bit. "Shall we play four square or tetherball?" Janet asked. So it was agreed that they'd play four square.

Missie joined in, of course. She had to learn how to play some of the games, since she'd been living overseas for quite some time. But she caught on fast, and they all had fun.

"Where exactly did you live overseas, Missie?" asked Elaine. "Seems like you told me, but now I've forgotten."

"Over in Africa. My dad was a mission doctor there."

"Africa? That's right. I remember now! By any chance have you heard of Timbuktu?"

"Yeah, I have," Missie said. "It's in Mali, I believe. We never went there, though."

Elaine was dumbfounded that Missie knew where this place was. She couldn't wait to tell her dad. "Wow!" she said. "Most people have never even heard of it, but my dad uses it as a word for a faraway place."

Missie laughed. "Then he's like my dad, who says 'Patagonia' for a little-known, remote place. Sometimes he says he's gonna ship us to Patagonia if we don't behave. Of course, we know he's just kidding." The girls chuckled.

When it was time for geography class, Elaine became acquainted with Elder Holford. He was a tall man with a friendly smile. His head was somewhat bald, but he didn't look old—not old the way Grandpa did.

His eyes sparkle, and he seems happy—even snappy, Elaine thought to herself. And she had him pegged right. He really was snappy. Not grouchy or ill-tempered, but quick-witted and clever. During a break he came to Elaine and said, "I understand from the principal that you're related to Dr. Steve Vitrano."

"You're right, Elder Holford. He's my uncle, my mom's brother. Do you know him?"

"I sure do. Your uncle Steve and aunt Charlene served as missionaries with us in India."

"Really? That's a surprise!" Elaine's face reflected her shock.

"They're good people. We enjoyed them so much."

"How nice" was about all she could think of to say. But when school was over for the day, Elaine ran out to the car where Mom and Marcia were waiting for her. She started jabbering away.

"What a fun first day! We laughed and talked, and everyone's nice. We agreed that we like playing four square and tetherball."

"I'm glad for you, Elaine," said Mom.

"I already told Mom that Miss Bassham is the best teacher I ever have had," Marcia said. Her eyes twinkled with excitement.

But Elaine could hardly contain herself. "Excuse me, Marcia, but I have some interesting news for you. Missie Ross knows about Timbuktu and where it is."

Marcia began to laugh. "You gotta be kidding."

"No. I'm not. Isn't that the strangest coincidence?"

"Wait till we tell Dad," said Marcia laughing.

Mom chuckled too and expressed her surprise. Excitedly Elaine continued, "Elder Holford is one of my teachers. He told me after geography class that he knew Uncle Steve and Aunt Charlene real well."

"What?" asked Mom. "How's that?"

"He and Mrs. Holford were missionaries in India when Uncle Steve and Aunt Charlene were there!"

"Well, can you beat that? I'm going to call Steve this evening and tell him about it." There was excitement in Mom's voice.

"He shook my hand real friendly-like. The girls stood next to me and listened to what he said. They told me later that they really liked him and that all the kids do. He won't tolerate any foolishness, but he's real good-natured. He said it was a pleasure to meet me, and he said he looked forward to getting better acquainted with our family."

"How nice!" said Mom. "Now I can't wait to visit with him myself."

❦

According to Elaine, Miss Crider was absolutely stupendous. She was a good teacher and took a personal interest in each student. It was her practice to invite one student every month or so to go to the public library with her to help select books to take back to school for the students to read.

This special project had made a real difference to a boy named Clyde during the past school year. He had never enjoyed school. He wasn't a dummy, but he was downright disagreeable, often sullen, and he could be mean. But Miss Crider turned him around so that he became a polite, happy, genial boy. All the kids in the room saw it happen. It was remarkable to watch their teacher's skill transform a boy right in front of their eyes.

"Come on, Clyde, let's give the gals a run for their money at recess time. We'll beat them at four square till they won't know what's happening," shouted the boys. And so it went during the rest of recess.

Of course, the study of geography was made all the more interesting when Elder Holford described the places he had lived and the others he had visited and the fascinating things he'd seen. He made geography come alive.

One day on a geography quiz one of Elder Holford's questions was to name the capital of a north German state they had been studying. Most of the kids looked puzzled and gazed up at the ceiling trying to remember.

So he gave them a clue. "It's the largest seaport in continental Germany." That didn't seem to help too much, so he said, "Think of something to eat." Then most of the students laughed and picked up their pencils.

But this hint did not help Elaine. She still didn't know the answer. Fretting and fuming, she probed her memory and scoured her brain. *Something to eat. H'mmmm. Something German. What could it be? Sauerkraut? No, that's not it.* In hopelessness she almost gave up. Then suddenly she remembered that every day they went by a little eatery on their way to school, and it served fast-food German style. In desperation she wrote the name of the restaurant, Der Wienerschnitzel.

When Elder Holford handed back the corrected quiz papers the next day, he stopped at Elaine's desk and began to laugh.

"Elaine, your answer tops anything I have ever seen," he said, pointing to question 5. "It's the wrong answer, but it was a *great* try. I gave you half a point."

Elaine's face argued with itself—whether to be glad or sad. But Elder Holford was smiling. "The answer was Hamburg. It's the largest seaport," he told her. Then he told the kids what Elaine had written, and they all giggled and laughed. "Even though she didn't get the right answer, she was thinking," he said, "and that's very important."

"Way to go, Elaine!" cheered Terry.

"Yeah, Elaine. Good one," laughed Nick.

And Elaine couldn't help feeling a bit smug about her cleverness.

Playing soccer that day during recess, Terry called, "Watch it, wienerschnitzel girl," when he kicked the ball toward Elaine. She didn't mind the teasing, especially when Terry and Nick told her she was a great kicker for a girl. Their team won, so that made Elaine feel good too.

After school on a windy, cloudy October day Joanie walked down the street to Elaine's house, bouncing a tennis ball all the way. She was dressed warmly, and her blue-and-white stocking cap bounded up and down, keeping time with the tennis ball. She and Elaine had made plans to play together. Cindy couldn't join them because she had a cold, and Monica had refused their invitation because she wanted to play with the new cat she'd received as a birthday present. Also, she always said she didn't like being with Joanie, Elaine, and Cindy and playing their *measly* games, as she called their make-believe fun.

We shouldn't have even asked her, Joanie thought, giving the ball an extra-hard bounce. They'd asked her just to be polite. Her mom said they shouldn't leave her out, but she wasn't fun to have around. She teased in a mean way and had to be first in everything.

"*Puuuuh*," Joanie puffed, feeling mad at Monica all over again.

The chilly wind blew her stocking cap across her face, and she brushed it aside. Though it was cold outside, she was dressed warmly. And pretty soon she'd be in Elaine's toasty-warm house.

Two weeks ago the autumn leaves had blazed red, orange, and gold, but now most of the branches were bare. Some of the birds had already flown south. Occasionally she heard the honking of Canadian geese flying high overhead, migrating to warmer weather.

"You better hurry, all you geese. Winter is on its way," ordered Joanie. She stopped to look up and watch a wavering V of geese against the clouds. It was then she first heard a muffled cry. "Ooooo, help me!"

Joanie stopped in her tracks. Her head jerked around, trying to find the sound. *What was that?* she wondered.

"Ooooooo! Help!"

There it was again.

That's coming from Monica's, I think. So, tennis ball in hand, Joanie walked quickly to the fence behind Monica's house.

"Help me! Somebody! Anybody!" Sure enough, it was Monica calling. Joanie stopped. Now she could see

121

Monica lying in a crooked heap in a thicket of brush on the ground.

"Monica, what happened?" she asked, quickly kneeling down beside her.

Big tears filled Monica's eyes and joined those on her dust-streaked cheeks. "I tried to get up, but I can't."

For the smallest moment Joanie thought of all the mean things Monica had said to her. For the shortest heartbeat she thought that it would serve the big bossy girl right if she just walked away. Joanie was naturally quiet and shy, and Monica had hurt her feelings many times. She had teased Joanie and called her a baby. She'd made fun of her hair and her clothes. And now she lay on the cold ground, caught by the intertwined vines and branches of the thicket. There were scratches on her arms, and a gash on her face oozed blood. One arm lay at a strange angle, as if it were broken.

Joanie blinked and mentally chased all those thoughts away. In a flash she knew she must do something. Her sweet but timid heart would not allow her just to walk away.

"Here, let me help you," she said, bending down. "You're all twisted up in those old vines." Kneeling down, she went to work clearing away the dead leaves, the dry prickly twigs, and other autumn foliage.

This was a time when goodness and strength of character overruled pettiness—even in the heart of a shy, timid child who had never heard one word of kindness from the mouth of the girl now lying helplessly on the ground.

"Ooooww, my arm is killin' me!" Monica wailed. One look at her face told Joanie that she was telling the truth.

Reaching down, little Joanie summoned all the strength she could muster. Carefully but slowly she took hold of Monica's good arm and pulled her. There was a lot of moaning and some screams, but finally Monica was on her feet. She wobbled a bit and almost fell down.

"Here, lean on me," Joanie said. "I'll help you to your house. What happened? How long have you been out here?"

"Seems like an hour," Monica groaned. "I'm freezing." She leaned against Joanie, staggering, and Joanie held her up.

"You came along in the nick of time. It was all Ginger's fault. She's my new cat, you know. I just got her for my birthday. She climbed up that pear tree in the backyard and then meowed and cried 'cause she didn't seem to know how to get down."

"I've heard of cats doing that," said Joanie as they slowly made their way to Monica's back door.

Monica stopped, leaned against Joanie, and tossed her hair back from her face. "I ran out to climb up the tree and rescue her, but it's the dumbest thing I ever did. Ginger wouldn't even let me touch her. She scratched my face with her claws. I musta jumped back, because the next thing I knew, I was falling. I landed on the ground with a crash." With a moan, she took another step. Joanie saw that she was limping and that shivers shook her body.

For the first time since she'd met Monica, Joanie was

the strong one of the two. Monica was helpless, and they both realized it.

"I almost didn't hear you," Joanie told her. "I couldn't make out what the sound was, and I was about to walk on. Then I heard you call again."

By now they were at Monica's back door. She paused, then seemed to pull herself up the first step. Inside they heard her mother's heavy footsteps coming toward the door. A moment later the woman yanked it open. A TV blared in the background.

"What's troublin' you now, you big baby? I thought I heard ya yowling out back somewhere." The woman glared at Monica but didn't waste a glance on Joanie.

Turning to Joanie, Monica smiled weakly and softly said, "Thanks."

"Git in here," the mother grumped, pulling her daughter into the house.

Joanie turned on her heel and hurried away. She could hear Monica crying and her mother yelling at her. She couldn't wait to get out of earshot.

But even as she half ran the rest of her way to Elaine's house, a new thought bounded through her mind. *So that's why Monica's so mean. Her mother is mean. My mom wouldn't treat me like that if I was hurt . . . Elaine's mom doesn't act like that.* And then she had a thought that astounded her.

Maybe Monica doesn't even know how to be nice.

Joanie couldn't wait to tell Elaine about Monica's accident and how she'd helped her. She started telling it as soon as she walked through the door. First, however, she patted Fritzie's head. He gave her a friendly wag of his puffy tail and gently licked her fingers. Joanie had no dog of her own, and she dearly loved Fritzie.

When she finished telling of Monica's accident, Elaine asked, "Were you scared, Joanie?"

"I wasn't scared of Monica. You should've seen her there on the ground. She looked awful," Joanie said. "But I was definitely scared of her mother!"

The next day the girls learned that Monica had truly broken her arm, for she now wore a cast. And as the weeks went by, Elaine and Joanie began to see little changes in her. It wasn't much at first, just that she didn't scowl at them all the time as she had before. And by the time her cast came off, Monica had started showing a genuine interest in Joanie. It seemed that there had come a turning point in Monica's young life. Apparently an impression had been made in her innermost soul. She seemed to sense the right and wrong of people's personal actions.

The change didn't happen at once, but it was a change nonetheless. Joanie told Elaine that she and Monica didn't become best friends right away, but Monica no longer belittled and teased her. Because of the kindness Joanie had shown her, something changed in Monica. She still ran around with her rough-and-tumble friends, but if she ever knew of any situation in which Joanie needed help, Monica was there. She was quick to put in a good word for her. In fact, at times she was Joanie's defender.

ELEVEN

Snow War

Elaine could hardly believe that the school year was slipping by so quickly. It seemed as though it had just begun. But the days became cooler, and she knew that winter was on its way. The children spilled out of the school building one day, happy to be in the fresh air and sunshine. It was Friday, the end of the week.

Elaine ran to the car, where her mother and Marcia were waiting. She quickly climbed in and waved goodbye to her friends.

Twenty-eighth Street had five lanes of very busy traffic no matter what time of day. Just before the big bridge over the freeway they all heard a loud bang, and immediately the back wheel started to wobble. Providentially, there was time and room for Mom to ease the car from the left lane onto the narrow far-right shoulder.

Mom had the girls get out of the car and stand behind the guardrail for safety. She inspected the tire. "It is just plain flat, no doubt about it. We had a blowout," she told them. "I'll have to find a phone and call for road service."

But just then a yellow truck pulled up behind their car, and out jumped a man with a contagious smile. "Having

126

trouble, I see," he said as he pushed back his cap and scratched his curly blond hair. "Do you have a spare tire?"

When Mom opened the trunk, he took out the tools and went to work. In no time at all the tire was changed. The man stood up, dusted himself off, and said, "There you are, good as new."

Mom had her wallet ready. "Please let me pay you, sir, for your kindness and assistance. I don't know what we would have done without you."

The man put up his hands. "You don't owe me a thing, ma'am. I was just glad to help you out. I would hope someone would help me if I were in trouble." He smiled, gave a nod and a wave to the girls, then jumped into his truck and took off.

Marcia and Elaine got into the car, and Mom followed. She was flabbergasted by how quickly the man had arrived, changed the tire, then left. She was also relieved. She and the girls could go on home, and Dad would take care of the ruined tire later.

Mom started the engine. The yellow truck was just a few cars ahead of them when she merged into traffic. "Let's see what company that man works for," Mom suggested. "The name must appear on the side of the truck. Then we can call his employer and commend him for his kind deed."

All of them kept their eyes on the yellow truck. When it began to turn right on the cloverleaf approach to the freeway below, they were sure they would see the company name.

But just as suddenly as the truck appeared, it dropped out of sight in all the traffic. "I can't believe it!" exclaimed Mom. "Either I lost track of him or he simply vanished."

Both girls agreed. "I never took my eyes off that truck," explained wide-eyed Elaine. "He vanished into thin air!"

"He was there one minute and gone the next," added Marcia.

They drove on, speechless. "He was so nice and came along just when we needed him. Do you suppose he was an angel?" Elaine wondered aloud.

Marcia nodded soberly. "Our very own angel," she murmured.

"Oh, thank You, Lord, for watching over us," Mom prayed aloud.

And when they said their prayers that night, they again thanked God for sending help and for every angel that guarded them on the busy streets as they drove back and forth to school every day. Together they repeated Psalm 34:7: "The angel of the Lord encamps all around those who fear Him, and delivers them" (NKJV).

The experience was one that the girls never forgot.

Fall was unusually chilly that year. Elaine didn't know whether to be happy or sad. She did love winter, although she admitted to herself that she really liked warmer weather better. But in December when the snow began falling, Elaine was glad. She and Marcia loved making snow people, especially when Dad helped. They'd make snow angels, too, by lying flat in the snow and dragging and pulling their arms and legs back and forth, leaving an imprint that looked like an angel with wings.

It continued to snow every day or so until the weather forecasters predicted this year might have a record snow-fall.

The family was first shocked and then laughed to see Fritzie take his first walk in the snow. Quite agilely he walked on his two front feet for a few short steps whenever he went outside. It seemed that he did not want to get all four of his feet wet. Fritzie was a natural-born athlete. That night for supper he got a special doggie treat. He probably didn't understand why or what he had done to deserve it, but he readily accepted it anyway and licked his chops. Oh, what a wonderful dog Fritzie was.

That winter Cindy, Joanie, Monica, and Elaine built a small fort at the end of the street down in the park. What fun they had pretending they were princesses who lived in an ice castle. At other times they were the soldiers who protected the castle. As snowballs flew back and forth, they'd run behind trees for protection. Finally, they'd fall into the snow, laughing and exhausted.

Monica seemed to fit in more now since she'd experienced a bad fall and broken arm. She wasn't always great to play with, but at least she was tolerable most of the time.

The day that Jeff and Davy came to inspect the fort, they threw back their heads and laughed. How they teased the girls.

"We'd better be careful, or those girl guards'll put us in jail inside their goofy fort!" Jeff yelled to Davy.

"Oooo, I'm scared. Those gals are tough soldiers," Davy cried, clowning around and pretending to be shaking with fear.

Elaine had turned her attention to watch the fun when a snowball hit her arm. Then another one sailed over her head and hit Cindy. Suddenly everyone was throwing snowballs, laughing when they were hit and laughing when they made a hit. But truth be told, the girls got hit more than the boys did. Everyone was jolly and joyful as they frolicked out in the afternoon sun.

Just then a big, black crow flew to the tall, leafless maple tree growing on the lane. It cawed above their heads in a loud, raucous voice.

Jeff looked up and called back to it, "You tell 'em, Gov'nor!"

Elaine laughed. The crows looked and acted as important as the black-robed officials she'd seen in the newspapers. Jeff was funny. He'd pegged that crow just right.

Davy pretended to be playing baseball. He wound up like a pitcher and threw a snowball straight as an arrow toward the trunk of the maple tree.

"Strike one!" yelled Jeff as the snowball splattered against the trunk. The big, black crow cawed his agreement.

"OK, umpire!" Davy yelled, looking up at the crow. "You call 'em."

"Here come the queen's female guards from London. Be careful!" Jeff shouted.

The girls snapped up that challenge. The war was on! They had the time of their lives teasing, howling, and yelling as they confronted the guys with snowball after snowball. But it was no use. The four girls were no match for two older boys.

At last the guys tired of the battle and turned to trudge home. But the girls continued to run and play until they were breathless.

TWELVE

Mysterious Tracks in the Snow

The very next Sunday morning the family traveled down to Uncle Steve's. The weather forecast was not good, but Aunt Gen and Uncle Bob were visiting from California, and with them were their two grown sons, Don and Rick. No one wanted to miss out on the family reunion. They were especially celebrating Don's safe return from Vietnam. Grandma and Grandpa would go back to California with Aunt Gen after the reunion.

"Tell us about Aunt Gen and her boys," Elaine said to Mom as the family rode along in the car on their way to Uncle Steve's. "Even though they're our cousins, I don't know much about them."

Elaine had heard her mother's stories about Aunt Gen, Uncle Bob, and their boys when they lived on their farm in Milton Junction, Wisconsin. But she had been very young when Aunt Gen's family moved to southern California. Years had gone by, and even though Aunt Gen often sent books and lovely clothes to Elaine and Marcia, they had never had a chance to get acquainted with either her or their cousins.

"Don was born when I was 15 years old," Mom began,

"and I thought he was the best baby that had ever landed on the face of the earth. I sang songs to him and played with him. He even told me once that he didn't have to mind me 'cause I was just a kid. I laughed and grabbed him and kissed him.

"He was an avid reader. Aunt Gen taught both her sons to read before they went to school. Why, when Don was only 5 years old, he knew how much an elephant weighed and how much a blue whale weighed. And he was surprised when grown-ups didn't know all he knew about animals and their habits." Mom laughed at the memory. "The child was simply amazing," she said.

"I don't think *I* know how much an elephant weighs," Elaine said slowly. *What did an elephant weigh, anyway?*

"Well, that was important to Don," Mom replied, "so he remembered it."

"What else did he do?" Marcia asked.

"Oh, so many things. He was a sweet little boy. And when he was 4, his brother, Rick, was born."

"Wow, I wish we had a baby cousin," Marcia sighed.

"It would be fun," Elaine agreed.

"It surely was," Mom said. "Rick was the boy who could sing like an angel. When I caught the mumps, Rick sat on my bed and sang 'Jesus Loves Me.' He sang all three stanzas by heart, to help me feel better. Then both Don and Rick caught the mumps from me.

"Rick was as sweet as the day was long. And he was a climber. One time Don called, 'Help, Mother. Come quick.' Aunt Gen found Rick sitting on top of her upright piano.

"Another time she went outside just in time to see Rick about halfway up the silo. Now, that was a very dangerous thing to do. Very calmly she walked to the bottom of the silo and talked him down. She didn't want to frighten him, only encourage him to take his time and descend safely."

Dad looked over at Mom. "I'm glad we had girls," he laughed. "That would have been too much for me!"

"Aunt Gen and Uncle Bob weren't surprised that Rick chose to major in PE in college," Mom said. "He was always athletic."

"Ed's majoring in PE too, isn't he?" Elaine asked.

"Yep," said Mom. "Both Ed and Rick are athletically talented."

Elaine and Marcia thought their big cousins were super. Joyce and Edwin, Don and Rick—they were celebrities to the girls. Of course, Roger was even more special. He was a kid, the same as them—a mighty good kid. They loved him.

The car fell silent. Dad was concentrating on driving, and Mom looked out the window, watching the fields go by. Silently Elaine mulled over in her mind the idea of war.

"Don was in a war, a *real* war, wasn't he?" she asked her mother. "Was he on the battlefield?"

"Yes," Mom replied. "He was a radio teletype operator."

Elaine shuddered just to think of the words "battlefield" and "war." *My cousin was in a real war.*

❦

As they pulled in to Uncle Steve's driveway, Roger ran out of the house to greet them.

"Hi, everybody!" he called. "Hi, Elaine. Hi, Marcia. Come on in."

What a grand time everyone had hugging and laughing with each other. *Grandpa does look older*, Elaine noticed. He wasn't crippled or anything, but he did move slowly. Yet his eyes shone with happiness, and his smile was still the same. Grandma was slim and well dressed, as always. She looked some older, too, but not nearly as much as Grandpa. He seemed smaller and . . . slower, maybe. Elaine couldn't quite figure it out. *Maybe it's just my imagination. Since Mom speaks so often of them both growing old, maybe I'm beginning to take notice.* Thoughts were churning in Elaine's head. She hugged Grandpa tightly and a little longer than she usually did.

Turning her attention to Grandma, Elaine could agree with Mom, who always said that Grandma had good taste and that Grandpa called her "graceful."

I can see why Grandpa was attracted to her. Elaine smiled an inward smile and wondered if any of the boys at school ever considered *her* graceful. Realistically, however, she figured that the thought had never entered their heads. But they did admire the way she could run—faster than any other girl in school, as they'd told her one time.

Roger urged the girls to come downstairs and see his new Ping-Pong table. They hit the ball back and forth for a while, but soon they were back with the grown-ups. None of them wanted to miss anything.

Everyone sat in the living room, even the big cousins. Extra chairs had been brought into the room, and some people even sat on the floor. Every so often Aunt Charlene and Aunt Gen went to the kitchen to check on dinner. It wasn't time to eat yet, but they wanted to keep an eye on the food. Joyce turned to Elaine and said, "Come, sit here by me. I can't get over how grown-up you're getting. And Marcia's growing up before my eyes too. Look at her there next to Grandma. She's a doll."

Elaine smiled as Joyce pulled her up close. Joyce was cool. She knew just what to do with her hair, and she dressed smartly. Elaine wished she could be just as stylish when she grew up.

Aunt Gen, Mom, and Uncle Steve dominated the conversation. Brother and sisters—they talked a mile a minute. When some point of adventure couldn't be re- membered quite right, Grandma or Grandpa straightened them out.

But poor Dad, Aunt Charlene, Uncle Bob, and the kids! All they could do was listen and laugh at the tricks and escapades and other funny things they were hearing. Quiet and soft-spoken, Uncle Bob was a well-mannered gentleman with a good sense of humor. What a hearty laugh he had when hearing the funny stories. He'd grown up on a farm near the small town of Milton Junction, Wisconsin, so his childhood and youth were far different from the stories being told. But kids are kids no matter where they live, and Uncle Bob could identify with some of the shenanigans they described.

So could Aunt Charlene. As a teacher she'd lived around schools all her life, and her parents had taught at both Battle Creek and Broadview academies. She'd grown up around high school students and had seen lots of kids clowning around.

Of course, some of the memories they talked about were serious or wistful or sad, but those were few and far between. Quite naturally the conversation turned to the unusually harsh winter weather the Midwest was currently experiencing. Then in quiet, thoughtful reflection Uncle Steve began telling about the winter he spent with Aunt Annie and Uncle Reynolds Stern up in New London, Wisconsin, where he had attended eighth grade in the church school that cousin Daisy Stern taught.

"It was just before we moved from Chicago to Milwaukee," he recalled.

"Yes, Steve," said Grandpa. "We knew we would be moving, and rather than having you and Gen change schools in the middle of the year, we had you go to Aunt Annie's in New London. They had a nice church school there." He paused, thinking. "The school was attached to the back of the old New London church, and you did not object—not one whit. How you loved that farm."

Aunt Gen spoke up. "And I went to stay with Aunt Daisy in Berrien Springs and attended academy. It was such fun. You'll remember that I didn't object either. Cousin Rachel and I were real pals."

"It was a crackerjack of a winter," Uncle Steve continued, and everyone settled back to listen to his story. "Lots of snow and cold. A typical Wisconsin winter." Then he stopped, shaking his head. "No, it was not typical. It was wicked. Uncle Reynolds and Dell said it was one of the worst they could remember."

"Did you sled and ice-skate a lot?" Roger asked.

"Sledding, yes, but ice-skate? I don't remember much skating. This was a long time ago, you must keep in mind," Uncle Steve explained with a smile. "I don't remember every detail."

"We know how old you are, Steve," teased Aunt Gen.

"Well, you're older than I am, don't forget!"

The laughter and joking almost ended.

"OK, already," said Edwin finally. "Get on with the story, Steve."

All the kids chimed in with "Yeah! Go on."

"Well, this occurred on a winter's day as we were driving home from school in Daisy's car," Uncle Steve began. "It could have been a calamity. That it wasn't is a puzzle to this day," he said, a faraway look in his eyes.

Even the big cousins were getting interested. "Did you have an accident or something?" asked Don.

"Seems now that I *do* recall your telling us about some danger you were in," Aunt Gen said. "Years ago."

"What happened?" asked Aunt Charlene. "I don't think I've ever heard you talk about this before." Everyone's eyes were riveted on Uncle Steve as he proceeded.

"It's been so long ago, well more than 30 years. I may not have every fact correct, but as I recall, Ginny, Carol, Daisy, and I were riding home after school one winter afternoon in Daisy's old car. It had snowed terribly a day or two before, and the roads weren't real good. Barely passable is about all you could say to describe them, those old country roads. Some dumb fellow who was driving too fast—considering the road conditions—passed us so closely that it forced Daisy to steer the car to the right so that we wouldn't get hit. As he passed us, snow flew and blew up into the air, and for a moment we could hardly see. Then a drift of snow stopped our car dead in its tracks. We were *really* stuck. There was no getting out."

"Did he see what his reckless driving caused? Could he see that you got stuck?" Rick asked.

"Probably not," answered Uncle Steve. "At least he didn't stop to help us. So Daisy decided we should walk back toward town and telephone Dell to come pull us out. We slogged through the snow, and poor little Carol and Ginny fell a couple times as we walked, getting their leggings and their mittens wet. The snow was so deep that it was up to their knees. It was miserable. We stayed inside the store while we waited.

"It didn't take Dell long to come to our rescue. A neighbor man came with him, and they had shovels. We went back to the scene of the accident. Dell and the neighbor had started in working when a fellow in an old jalopy of a car—worse than ours—came by. He offered to take the girls and Daisy home. I remember Carol crying that she didn't want to go with the man.

"But from what I can recall, both Dell and Daisy felt it was best, so Daisy and the girls climbed into the car and took off with the old but friendly codger. I stayed with Dell.

"It didn't take terribly long before we got the car unstuck, and with great relief we started for home again. When Dell turned in at the farm, he drove directly into the shed next to the corncrib there, just as he always did."

"I know right where that corncrib was," Grandma said.

"I do too," Aunt Gen agreed, and Grandpa nodded.

"But I saw a puzzled look come over Dell's face," Uncle Steve said. "It was obvious that Dell was baffled about something. I asked him what it was that bothered him, and he answered that he could see car tracks going right up to the house, but there seemed to be no tracks of the car leaving. We wondered if the man was still there. I walked around inspecting the one-way tracks, and Dell was right. We hurried into the house, hoping that all was well with the girls.

"Well, everyone was there and OK, and we all hugged each other, and then Dell began to ask questions. 'Was the fellow nice and polite? Did you know him?' Questions like that.

"Daisy shrugged her shoulders and said they didn't know him. They'd never seen him before, but he was a kind man and had driven them right to the house. She said that he seemed to know them.

"Now, I remember," Uncle Steve continued, "that spunky, never-bashful Ginny spoke up just then. She explained that she'd leaned forward from the back seat and tried to tell the fellow where they lived. She was going to give him some directions to the house, but he said he already knew where they lived. And he drove that old ramshackle car right up to the house, talking in a friendly way all the time. He mentioned people they knew and different family members. Daisy figured he must have known Dell from somewhere."

Don spoke up. "He knew where they lived without them telling him?"

"That's right," Uncle Steve replied. "That's not so strange when you live in a real small town. But what happened next *is* very strange. They had all waved goodbye to him and heard his car engine start, and heard him drive away. At least they thought they did, but no one looked out the windows to see what direction he went. They were too busy talking to Aunt Annie and Uncle Reynolds, telling them about being stuck and all. They paid no attention to the man after he walked out the door."

"Who was he, anyway?" Ed asked.

"Dell didn't know," Steve replied. "He'd never seen him before as far as he could remember, and *I* sure didn't know the guy. We were all dumbfounded. Everyone looked blankly at the other person, trying to figure it all out.

"I remember that Carol spoke up and told her dad that she was scared to ride with the man because she'd been told not to ride with strangers. She said that she'd cried, so Daisy held her on her lap all the way home.

"Dell put his arm around his little daughter and hugged her. All of us realized that it could have, indeed, been a serious mistake to accept this man's offer of assistance. But it was Dell who pointed out something that has kept me thinking to this very day.

"'How come there are tire tracks leading *to* the house but not *away* from it?' Dell asked. 'The man would have had to turn around *somewhere*.' The puzzled, concerned look on Dell's face worried us all. Almost in a whisper he said, 'I just don't understand it.'

"Immediately, inquisitive Ginny flew to the door, grabbed her jacket, slid into her boots, lit a lantern, and ran outside. She didn't even stop to pull on her cap. I got up to watch out the window to see where she went. After she ran around the house, she came back in, wagging her head, and breathlessly announced, 'You're right, Dad. There are no tire tracks leading *away* from the house. They just stop at the door and go nowhere else. How come?'

"'I dunno,' Dell said. 'It wasn't snowing today, so it wasn't snow that covered the tracks. He couldn't possibly have driven in reverse in the exact same tracks, so he would have had to circle around somehow. We would have seen evidence of that.'

"We were stunned into silence," Uncle Steve said. "Who could this man have been?

"After a bit, Aunt Annie finally stood up and told us to come to the table for supper. Everything was ready. She had made her delicious cream of tomato soup and served fresh-baked bread with it, and cheese. 'Baked apples for dessert,' she told us.

"Well, we quickly sat down to eat. Growing boy that I was, I was famished. Soup, bread, cheese, and baked apples! Wow, was I ready! When Uncle Reynolds said grace, he fervently thanked the good Lord for sending an angel to help us get home, and we all said a fervent amen. We surely meant it."

As Uncle Steve finished his story, there was silence. Everyone thoughtfully looked out the window or down at the floor, slowly but surely grasping the significance of what they had just heard.

Joyce hugged Elaine up closer.

Then Grandma spoke up. With awe in her voice she said, "It seems as though now I do remember that story," she said. "Annie told me, but I'd forgotten all about it. It *had* to have been an angel."

"God is so good to all of us," Grandpa remarked reverently. "We must always remember how He leads us. This remarkable story illustrates divine intervention."

Everyone agreed—both kids and grown-ups.

THIRTEEN

Family Portrait

After a moment Aunt Charlene broke the silence. "Let's eat," she said. "We're having spaghetti, and I used Grandpa's recipe for the tomato sauce. Gen made Grandpa's garbanzo meatballs."

Elaine slid into a chair next to Joyce at the huge dining table, and Rick slid into the chair at the end of the table next to Elaine. Grandma and Grandpa were right across from them.

"Grandma told me about your swimming lessons, Elaine," said Rick. "I love swimming too." He gave her a quick smile and wink.

"You do?" Elaine asked. Her innermost young heart beat with a feeling of satisfaction and a bit of pride that Rick was noticing her and her swimming accomplishment.

"We're a lively bunch of cousins, Elaine. You fit right in with the rest of our active family. It's in the blood, you know. We're cut from the same pattern."

Elaine chuckled. She'd never thought of cousins being cut from a family pattern. The idea tickled her imagination. *He's so good-looking,* she thought, *and full of fun, too. Wow!*

Uncle Steve quieted everyone down so that he could

144

have Grandpa say the blessing. "We don't want to behave like the heathen, do we, Dad?" he asked. His eyes twinkled with mischief. Grandpa was the one who would say "We're no better than the heathen" if the family forgot to say grace.

Grandpa chuckled. "That's right. Let's bow our heads."

After the blessing, Aunt Charlene said, "Let's eat," and she began passing the food. In between bites, Elaine said, "Mom says you like music, Rick, and that when you were only 4 or 5 years old, you sat on her bed and sang to her to help cheer her up when she had the mumps."

"Yeah, that's right. But I caught the mumps from that singing performance," Rick chuckled. "What a reward! Doesn't seem fair, does it?" Again he laughed. "But the price wasn't so high that it discouraged me from loving music."

"I like music too," Elaine answered. "Aunt Gen—I mean, your mom—sent me and Marcia a set of records for Christmas a couple years ago. There are fun songs on it, and we play them a lot. I like the Davy Crockett music and 'Seventy-six Trombones.' I think that's from *The Music Man*. Oh, yes, I just love 'Do-Re-Mi' from *The Sound of Music*. Do you think that liking music is a piece of the family pattern?" she asked playfully. A glint of laughter lit her eyes. She liked the pattern idea.

"Definitely, definitely, Elaine," Rick laughed. "The love of music is our inheritance. Both Grandma and Grandpa passed this along to us." He pointed across the table, and Grandma nodded.

"Mom told me long ago about your being left-handed," Elaine said. "She says we have quite a few left-handed people in our family tree."

Rick nodded and laughed with his lips closed, his cheeks bulging. His mouth was full of food. After he swallowed a big gulp he said, "See where I'm sitting right now, at this end of the table? I usually sit at this spot so that my left hand has enough room to move around. I've learned to adjust to it, though, and can sit anywhere around any table now. But I found it inconvenient when I was a kid." Then looking across the table to Grandma, he said, "Our grandma heard me fuss about being left-handed, so she told me that the Bible tells of King David having a special group of left-handed soldiers—very good, highly respected soldiers—who that could 'throw to a hair's breadth' because of their accuracy in taking aim. That made me proud. I even wonder if David was left-handed when he used his sling to kill Goliath."

Grandpa looked at Rick. "Well, David was from the tribe of Benjamin, and it was the Benjamites that were the left-handed experts. He could have been too. When we get to heaven, we'll ask David himself which hand he used." He paused, then continued. "Many excellent baseball pitchers are left-handed, Rick. Have you ever thought of that?"

"You're right, Grandpa. I knew that. And many good baseball players are Italian," Rick said, giving Grandpa a big grin.

What a feast everyone had. Spaghetti, garbanzo

meatballs, green beans, tossed salad with tomatoes served with Italian dressing seasoned with onions and sweet basil. They had fresh warm bread, and to top it all off, cheesecake for dessert. Even though it sometimes seemed that everyone talked at once, they ate happily as they talked, passing bowls of spaghetti and sauce for second helpings.

Grandpa's eyes twinkled with delight as he watched his granddaughter Marcia eat. "Look at the gusto that girl shows while eating spaghetti," he said with a proud smile. It was true. Marcia could keep up with the other kids when it came to spaghetti.

"I like pizza, too, Grandpa," she said between bites. "I hope there's pizza flavor on the tree of life."

Everyone laughed, and Grandpa laughed the loudest. Marcia looked puzzled, but she laughed too.

"Pizza flavor, Marcia?" Elaine repeated. "But the tree of life has fruit on it, not pizza." Elaine's eyes danced with merriment as she giggled.

"Right on, Marcia," agreed Mom. "I hope there's a chocolate flavor treat on the tree of life, too."

"So do I," laughed Grandma. "I just love Mounds bars."

"Maybe Jesus can make a peach that tastes just like pizza just for you, Marcia," said Grandpa. "Won't it be wonderful when we all get to heaven to have our heavenly Father hand Marcia something to eat from the tree of life. I can just hear Him say, 'Here, Marcia, have some pizza.' That will be a glorious day."

Sometime later Elaine found Don sitting in a chair gazing out the big picture window overlooking Uncle Steve's backyard. The yard sloped down to a pretty pond that was completely frozen over. The trees were frosted with ice and snow.

Don looked up and held out his hand. "Come join me, Elaine," he said. "It's been a long time since I saw you last." He pulled up the ottoman and, giving it a pat, invited her to sit down.

Jokingly, with a gleam in her eye, she asked, "Do you still know how much an elephant weighs?"

Don threw back his head and laughed. "About 10,000 pounds, as I recall. I see your mother has told you about me and my childhood interest in the animal kingdom. She and I had so much fun when I was little and she was young. Ooops, excuse me. I don't mean to imply she's old now. I'm just referring to my boyhood." There was a twinkle in his eye.

Elaine was amused. She knew what he meant. Then looking straight at him, she said, "I wondered if you might be wearing your Army uniform. I'll bet you looked spiffy."

Don laughed. "I left the uniform at home. I've worn it enough for now."

"You were in a real war, weren't you?" asked Elaine.

"Yes, I was in a real war."

"What did they make you do? Mom says you were a

radio teletype operator or whatever. How could they use radios out in the middle of a battlefield?"

"They were a special kind of radio, Elaine, a type of phone, so soldiers could talk to one another, even though they were some distance apart. Our battalion assignments were to place these special radios in strategic places for the companies in the fields to use when they needed to ask for information, or help, or medical evacuations."

"Oh, I get it," said Elaine. "Radios so they could talk to each other." Then she asked, "Did you get shot at?"

"No. And I'm glad I didn't. But once, after our battalion left one location and went to another, we learned the enemy shelled the place where we'd just been. War is not good. It is ugly." He was very serious.

Elaine sat spellbound. Don, indeed, was her hero.

Her visit with Don was interrupted by Uncle Steve announcing that a photographer would be arriving soon to take the family photo. Elaine understood it was an important occasion. With Grandma and Grandpa "getting on," a family photo would be one to cherish.

"Come, Elaine," Joyce invited as she took her cousin to her bedroom. "Would you like me to do your hair up special for the picture?"

"Oh, yeah." Elaine was excited. In her estimation, Joyce was groovy (as her pal Cindy would say). Joyce knew something about everything—from hairstyles to fashionable chic clothing. And she could sing like a lark.

Elaine had heard her sing during other family visits. She knew that Joyce sang solos in school, too.

"So you are going to step into Joyce's beauty parlor," teased Ed. He was tops on Elaine's list. She liked the way he teased her. He could take the basement steps three at a time in a flash, and not even Dad or Uncle Steve did that. He'd been president of his senior class at Andrews Academy, and Elaine could understand why. He was popular.

Joyce paid no attention to him but took Elaine by the hand, and away they went down the hall to her room.

For the family photograph, Elaine and Marcia wore the dark-blue velvet dresses with wide white collars that Aunt Gen had made for them. When everyone was ready, they all stood in front of the red-brick fireplace.

"OK now, who is who?" the photographer asked. He had placed four chairs right in the middle.

Jokingly Grandpa replied, "Since Grace and I are the youngest, we probably should sit here in the middle. Right?" He took Grandma's hand and had her sit next to him in the center chairs. Everyone chuckled.

"We're the daughters," Aunt Gen explained, "so don't we sit in the front row too?"

"Sure thing. You've got that right," the photographer said with a laugh. So Mom sat next to Grandma, and Aunt Gen sat next to Grandpa.

Looking at Elaine and Marcia, the photographer asked, "Whom do you belong to?"

Elaine pointed to Mom, so he had her and Marcia stand

on either side of Mom. When Steve said that he was the son in the family, he was placed right behind Grandpa.

"Now then," said the photographer with a glint in his eye, "who are the in-laws and the out-laws, and whose child are you?" He pointed at Roger.

Among all the laughter and moving in and around, everyone was finally in place—Dad stood behind Mom; Roger, Edwin, Joyce, and Aunt Charlene stood next to Uncle Steve; Uncle Bob, Don, and Rick stood behind Aunt Gen.

"Such a to-do," said Grandma quietly to Mom. They both chuckled softly. "But I'm sure it is worth it. I like his organization."

Grandpa was content just to sit quietly during all the bustle and commotion.

Finally it was over. "How good it is to have all our family together," said Grandma. Grandpa nodded. There was something in Grandpa's expression that spoke volumes. Elaine caught a glimpse of it, but wasn't sure how to explain it. She just knew she loved him and Grandma.

"Well, Elaine," said Grandma, "let's hear the conclusion of the whole matter." She chuckled. "For now, you and Marcia are the youngest members of our tribe. You're the end of the line. The last of our clan." She shook her head and grinned. "No matter how I say it, it doesn't sound complimentary."

"Yes, Mother," chuckled Aunt Gen. "Can't you do better than that?"

"The baby chicks of the brood," Uncle Steve suggested.

"That's no better," said Grandpa, slapping his knee and laughing.

"I worked on the farm too long, didn't I?" asked Uncle Steve.

"Why not just say that Elaine and Marcia are the youngest in their generation?" Aunt Gen recommended. She smiled and hugged her young nieces.

"As always, Gen," said Grandma, "you have the best last word."

FOURTEEN

Good Times End, but Heaven's Coming

 The good time ended far too soon for Elaine, but she knew they had to get home.

Grandma hugged Elaine and Marcia, saying, "Don't forget to write. We love your letters and the little cards you make. I keep them in an album so that Grandpa and I can look at them every now and then."

Grandpa's eyes glistened. He hugged and hugged everybody. He even started to hug Aunt Gen, and she wasn't leaving. How they all laughed at that.

"You're going home with me in a couple of days, Dad," Aunt Gen told him. "You don't have to hug me yet, but if you want to, I'll hug you back." Grandpa had already realized his mistake and was wagging his head and laughing.

Aunt Charlene handed Mom a covered plate of four small pieces of delicious leftover cheesecake. "Here's something to enjoy," she said. "Now, don't forget to call us as soon as you get home."

"That's right," agreed Grandma. "I'll sleep better knowing you arrived home safely."

So off Dad drove as Elaine and Marcia waved out of the back window until they couldn't see anyone anymore.

"My dad is looking so old," Mom said sadly as they drove along. "I'm so glad that they were able to fly out here and that we could have this time together."

But Elaine was thinking of something else. "I'd love to have seen Don in his uniform," Elaine said to no one in particular. She still had not gotten over her awe of Don, the soldier boy.

"Before we leave Berrien Springs," Dad said as he turned the car onto the highway, "let's make a quick stop at my folks' place. OK?" He looked at Mom.

"Of course," she said quickly. "They're right on the way out of town."

"I know we get to see them much more often than we see your parents," Dad said, "but we won't stay long. This will give us a chance at least to say hello."

Mom agreed. "That's a good idea," she said.

So Dad made a turn, and soon they rolled into his parents' driveway. Everyone pulled their coats around them and hurried up the walk to the house. Just like at Uncle Steve's, snow covered the lawn, but someone had shoveled the sidewalk, and it was clear of snow. Dad rang the doorbell, and a moment later a surprised Grandma Clara met them at the door.

"Oh, my dear! What a surprise. Where did you come from?" she said, opening the door and all but pulling them into the warm house. "Hurry. Come in out of the cold." And each of them, Mom and Dad, Marcia and Elaine, got a big hug before they went any further.

"Louis," Grandma Clara called between hugs, "look

who's here." And Grandpa Louis joined them and led the way into the living room. And there—surprise of all surprises—they found Aunt Debbie with a guy they had never seen before.

Aunt Debbie was the youngest in Dad's family and had been only 3 years old when Dad and Mom married. Elaine and Marcia loved to look at their wedding pictures and think about Mom and Dad before they themselves were born. Mom had told them about cute little Debbie, their flower girl, and how she slowly walked down the aisle with cousin Rick, the Bible boy. She looked adorable in the wedding photos, but the girls thought their grown-up Aunt Debbie was even prettier than she'd been then.

Aunt Debbie stood right up to meet them. A big smile was on her face. "Come," she said. "I would like to introduce you to my friend Ken."

Ken had a friendly smile as he shook hands with Mom and Dad. Then he looked at Elaine and Marcia and said, "Hi, girls. It's nice to meet ya!"

So Aunt Debbie and Ken shared a few words with them all. Grandma Clara was urging everyone to sit down and asking if they'd like some hot chocolate, but Dad said they didn't even have time to sit down.

Explaining that they'd spent the afternoon with Mom's family because *her* mom and dad were visiting from California, he said, "We've got to be on our way home. I want to stay ahead of the weather that they say is coming our way from Chicago, but I couldn't drive by and not say howdy to everyone. Is there any more news about the weather?"

"No," said Grandma, "except that we're expecting more snow."

"Nothing new there," Ken said, and everyone agreed.

"We got a phone call from Norman yesterday," Grandpa told Dad. "He said he was going to be flying to Pennsylvania to pick up a small plane for his boss and fly it back to Idaho. Hope he doesn't have bad weather."

Elaine's uncle Norman, one of Dad's younger brothers, was a pilot out West in Idaho. He had graduated from college with a degree in business—the same as Dad—but Norman had also taken aviation classes. He learned to fly and to do mechanical work on airplane engines. After college he spent time in the Army's Operation Whitecoat. And when he finished his time in the Army, he took a job flying for a crop-dusting company out West.

"Keep us posted on his whereabouts," Dad said. The worry wrinkles in his forehead matched those in his father's.

So everyone hugged everyone again. Mom gave Aunt Debbie an extra hug and Ken a good handshake, and Aunt Debbie hugged the girls twice and kissed their cheeks. Grandma and Grandpa stood in the doorway watching them get into the car, waving as they drove off.

"Do you think they'll get married?" asked romantic Elaine as soon as they got into the car.

"Who?" Dad teased.

"Oh, Daddy. You know."

"Don't know," answered Dad, "but from the few minutes we spent with them, that Ken fellow appears to be a nice guy."

"He's handsome," Elaine said. Already she was dreaming of her own prince.

"Handsome isn't everything," Dad told her. "But, of course, I want Debbie to have a happy marriage."

"She's grown up to be a wonderful girl," Mom added. "Any man should be proud to have a wife like her."

His eyes on the highway, Dad nodded. "Debbie deserves a good husband. Naturally, I want the best for her."

"Be very careful about whom you marry, girls," Mom warned as she half turned so she could look at her daughters in the back seat. "My grandmother Marilla was known for advising her children to take care when deciding whom to marry. She often cautioned, 'If you marry the right person, your life together will be long enough. But if you marry the wrong person, it will be too long.'" She looked at both girls. "Do you know what she meant?"

Elaine and Marcia looked at each other and giggled. Those were serious words, and they understood the wisdom of them.

It started snowing several miles before they reached home, small flakes that flew right into the windshield and made it seem as though they were driving through a tunnel of snow. When Dad drove into their driveway, he breathed a sigh of relief. "Now, let it snow," he said. "Let it snow!" They had beaten the storm that came raging in later that night.

The first thing Elaine did was let Fritzie out for a run in the backyard. Then the girls cuddled him and hugged him, and he lovingly licked their faces. He was glad they were home.

Early the next morning, before Dad left for work, the phone rang. "Hello, Pa," they heard Dad say. He listened quietly for a moment, and then asked, "So he's OK for now?" There was another pause, then Dad said, "Oh, that's good. Let me speak to Norman."

Elaine and Marcia quietly ate their breakfast as Dad talked and talked and talked. His voice was so serious that it made them feel strange. At last they heard Dad say, "Keep me posted, Norm. Goodbye." And he hung up the phone with a sigh.

"Is Norman all right?" asked Mom.

"Yes, for now." Dad shook his head and sank into a chair by the table. "I've been concerned about him in this storm. I'm so relieved."

Mom sat down too. "What happened?"

"Well, as my dad told us, last week Norm's boss asked him if he'd be willing to go to Pennsylvania, pick up a single-engine plane the boss had purchased, and fly it back to Idaho.

"So Norm flew to Pittsburgh and looked the plane

over. He made several repairs that were necessary, and then he took off."

Both Marcia and Elaine had stopped eating, and were watching Dad as he talked.

"On his way back Uncle Norman ran into a very, very strong headwind, and the moist air caused ice to form on the plane. He said he was grateful he'd repaired the deicing equipment, and he flew on. But the storm got worse and became so fierce that the deicing equipment couldn't handle it. Uncle Norman knew then that he had to land the plane. But where?

"Fortunately, he was now here in Michigan, flying over Berrien County. He calculated that he was only 15 or 20 miles from our folks' house. It must have been hard for him to see through the window, but he spotted a small frozen lake, circled over it once to check it out, and landed."

Mom gasped. Her hand went to her throat.

Dad nodded. "You know, we have lots of small lakes, ponds, and lagoons here in Michigan, as well as the Great Lakes all around the state. It was getting dark, so he walked to a farmer's home and phoned Pa to come and get him."

They all sat in silence. Mom was shaking her head. Elaine quietly took it all in, then thoughtfully said, "Uncle Norman's guardian angel watched over him, don't you think?"

"Maybe his angel helped him fly the plane," said Marcia.

"You're right, girls," Dad replied. "I agree with you both."

Then he had to hurry off for work. The city snowplows had worked through the night, so the roads were clear. Mom took the girls to school, then did some grocery shopping on the way home. Off and on during the day she listened to the weather reports. Everything was "iffy," but snow was predicted for the next week.

"It seems that we'll definitely have a white Christmas this year," Mom said as she picked the girls up from school.

Two days later the phone rang after supper. It was Dad's father. After getting the news, Dad hung up and told his "girls" what he had learned. "This morning Uncle Norman went back to where he'd landed the plane. He inspected the plane. It wasn't hurt by the emergency landing and was still in good shape, and the field was OK for takeoff. He knew immediately that things were going to be favorable for flying—the weather, the ground, and the plane. So he took off and is on his way to Idaho.

"Apparently they didn't have as much snow in Berrien Springs as we had here, but that sure was a touch-and-go situation," Dad said. "I hope he never has to do that again."

What a relief the family felt.

On Friday evening, as they had sundown worship, Dad

said, "Won't it be wonderful when we all get to heaven? We'll get to meet Jesus and our guardian angels who have protected us during our lives, and we'll see the Holy City and the beautiful scenery and all the animals that are wild now but will be tame in heaven."

Elaine and Marcia nodded their heads.

"I wonder if we'll have snow in heaven," said Marcia.

"Maybe on some planet somewhere," said Elaine with a smile. "But I can't imagine snow around God's throne."

"Why not?" Marcia asked. "Snow is clean and beautiful."

Dad laughed. "We'll just have to be faithful and get there so we can see for ourselves," he said.

"And," added Mom, looking at Marcia, "we'll get to eat pieces of pizza-flavored goodies from the tree of life, and perhaps we will all get to swim in the river of life. Even *I* will know how to swim then!"

Marcia laughed when she added, "Ummm, pizza!"

"And Uncle Norman won't have to worry about flying in storms," said Dad. "He can fly safely to any planet he chooses—maybe with wings of his own!"

"And Grandpa will be able to climb up and down big mountains. His legs will be strong, and he won't be afraid of heights," said Mom, recalling the story Grandpa had told about his adventure up and down the mountain in Misilmeri.

"I think it would be fun if I could play the piano in heaven and accompany the angel choir," Elaine said thoughtfully.

"That's a wonderful idea, Elaine," Mom told her. She picked up her daughter's hand. She could hardly see the small, faded scars that had almost vanished from her fingers. "You can be a guest performer and play with the New Jerusalem Philharmonic. We'll all sit on the front row."

Elaine smiled.

"Yes, heaven will be a glorious place. Let's be sure to be there," said Mom. Elaine and Marcia nodded in agreement. Heaven would be better than they could even imagine.

Epilogue

No one knew the future, of course, but as it turned out it was a good thing that they'd had the family photo taken when they were together in Michigan. Only four months later Grandpa Justus passed away. How the family grieved.

The funeral was held in Berrien Springs. It was a special service led by Elder Tony Castlebuono along with two other associate pastors of Pioneer Memorial church. All the family loved Tony Castlebuono, and he provided a special link to the past. Many years before, Grandpa Justus had baptized him and his father.

Grandpa was buried in nearby Rose Hill Cemetery. Elaine had never attended a funeral before, and she didn't think she ever wanted to go to another one. She looked over at Grandma, and her heart felt heavy. Her heartfelt prayer was that Jesus would come very, very soon.

The Rest of Elaine's Story

Elaine attended Andrews University, where she majored in communicative disorders. After graduating from college, she earned a master's degree in speech pathology from Western Michigan University. It is interesting that Elaine graduated from the same schools that her father did—from academy through her graduate degree.

It was during college that Elaine met a young man by the name of Dann Hotelling. She thought that there was a lot to like about him, and he thought the same about her. After they were married, he earned a Master of Business Administration degree from the University of Michigan, and his new job took them to Cincinnati, Ohio.

Elaine and Dann have three children—Erin, Benjamin, and Bradley. While the family lived for a short time in both Arizona and New York when Dann was on assignment, their home is near Kettering, Ohio. When first married, Elaine worked as a speech pathologist, but after Erin was born she became a stay-at-home mom. Now she occasionally works as a substitute teacher. Erin, Benjamin, and Bradley attended Spring Valley Academy in Centerville, Ohio.

The family members love traveling and have visited many of the U.S. national parks. They especially enjoyed Yellowstone Park, where they saw beautiful wild animals such as bison, moose, elk, a little black bear (very close up), and in the far distance, grizzlies. Their favorites were the bison—big and slow, and close by.

More About Elaine's World

The world in which Elaine was born in 1961 was on the edge of big changes. In January of that year newly elected U.S. president John Kennedy moved into the White House. In a speech he said something that many people still remember: "Ask not what your country can do for you—ask what you can do for your country."

That year the Soviets sent the first man into space—and the race between the U.S.S.R. and the United States to conquer space was on. Both countries wanted to win. Kennedy made a goal to have a man on the moon—and back—before the end of the decade.

On May 5, 1961, Americans sent Alan Shepard into space. Then on February 20, 1962, John Glenn became the first American astronaut to circle the earth. He went around the earth three times.

In 1963 the Soviets put the first woman in space.

Americans walk on the moon

U.S. space exploration continued as quickly as possible. In 1968 the U.S. launched the first piloted space mission to orbit the moon. And in 1969 U.S. astronauts

Neil Armstrong, Edwin "Buzz" Aldrin, and Michael Collins reached the moon in their spacecraft. Armstrong was the first human to set foot on the moon. Buzz Aldrin followed, while Collins circled the globe before returning to get them. Then only a few months later, on November 19, two more men walked on the moon. The next day they successfully blasted off to rejoin their waiting astronaut in the command ship.

1963: Equal rights for all people

In 1963 Elaine was 2 years old.

Many people in the U.S. had become concerned that despite the fact that U.S. slaves had been freed nearly 100 years before, in some places Black people were still not allowed to eat where others ate. Black children were not allowed to go to White public schools. Black people had to sit in the back of public buses. And so in 1963 more than 200,000 people came to Washington, D.C., to march for equal rights for Blacks and Whites.

On August 28, 1963, Martin Luther King, a Black leader, gave a speech. He said that he had a dream that someday his own four children would not be judged by the color of their skin but by the content of their character.

On November 22, 1963, President Kennedy was assassinated. The tragedy shook the entire nation. Vice president Lyndon Johnson became the thirty-sixth president of the United States.

The next year, 1964, the U.S. passed the first civil

rights bill to stop discrimination against any people because of their race.

The Adventist Church kept up with the changing times. In 1965 the General Conference Committee voted a statement on human relations. It said that church membership and holding a church office must be open to any qualified person, regardless of race. And it said that in Adventist schools no teachers, staff, or students can be refused because of their race.

It can kill you

Something else interesting happened the next year. For the first time a warning was printed on packages of cigarettes. It said, "Caution: Cigarette smoking may be hazardous to your health."

In 1967, when Elaine was 6

The first handheld calculator was invented. You could buy one for "only" $2,500.

On December 3, 1967, a South African surgeon transplanted a human heart from one person (who had died in a car wreck) to another. The man who received the heart lived 18 days. He died of pneumonia.

The Seventh-day Adventist Church, 1970

The General Conference Committee passed an action to open doors for Black people to serve as leaders in church conferences and unions, and the General Conference.

The SDA Theological Seminary opened an archaeological museum. This was in Berrien Springs, on the campus where Elaine's uncle Steve taught. Several hundred items in the museum came from the Adventist archaeologist Siegfried H. Horn. In 1978 the museum was named the Siegfried H. Horn Archaeological Museum in honor of him. You can still visit it today.

A seminary is a training school for pastors and Bible teachers. It is what is called "graduate work," studies taken after you have graduated from college.

The "bigwig" who became president

In 1969 Richard Nixon became the thirty-seventh president of the United States.

That same year the U.S. Supreme Court ordered immediate school desegregation of 33 Mississippi school districts.

The next year, 1970, the U.S. Supreme Court set a deadline for the desegregation of public schools in several Southern states.

April 1, 1970, President Nixon signed a bill banning cigarette advertising on TV and radio. It went into effect the first day of 1971.

In 1972 President Nixon was reelected president of the United States.

On October 10, 1973, Nixon's vice president, Spiro Agnew, resigned after pleading "no contest" to the charge of income tax evasion.

On December 6, 1973, House minority leader Gerald

Ford was sworn in as vice president, replacing Agnew. Gerald Ford was the "bigwig" that Elaine and Marcia waved to at the parade in Grand Rapids.

And then on August 9, 1974, President Richard Nixon resigned.

On the same day, August 9, 1974, Vice President Gerald Ford took the oath of office, becoming the thirty-eighth president of the United States.

What was new back then?

Some of the things invented when Elaine was young may touch your life today. Look at these inventions. Do you use any of them?

1961: nondairy creamer
1962: Spacewar, the first computer game
1964: permanent-press fabric
1965: contact lenses
1968: computer mouse
1970: floppy disk
1972: word processor
1974: Post-it Notes
1979: Walkman

A Horse Called . . .

Meet five remarkable horses—Mayonnaise, Blackberry, Poppyseed, Tamarindo, and Saskatoon. As you read these exciting stories, you'll learn information that will help you earn Pathfinder honors in Horsemanship and Horse Husbandry.

Book One 0-8280-1131-1

Book Two 0-8280-1090-9

Book Three 0-8280-1307-1

Book Four 0-8280-1499-X

Book Five 0-8280-1562-7

WHAT WOULD YOU DO TO FIT IN?

JENNIFER WILL DO WHATEVER IT TAKES.

When Jennifer moves to Milwaukee, she finds herself in a new world of crushes, going steady, pranks, cheerleaders, and rebellion. As she struggles to launch from wallflower status to super-popular girl, she is sure that being cool will fill the emptiness within her. But as Jennifer's reality crashes down, it becomes clear that only God can fill the aching hole in her heart.

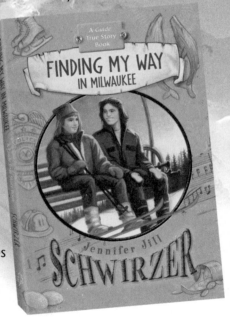

Paperback. 978-0-8127-1913-2.